Ghostly Images

A Harper Harlow Mystery Book Five

Lily Harper Hart

ONE

"Watch your hair!"

Zander Pritchett scorched his best friend Harper Harlow with a dark look, annoyance practically rolling off him in waves as he pressed his hand to the spot above his heart.

"Watch my hair?" Harper fought the urge to pinch Zander's flank, mostly because she would have to run twenty feet to accomplish it and an angry ghost separated the duo and offered mayhem if she tried. She wasn't worried about her hair – er, well, not much. She was more worried about avoiding the furious ghost zipping back and forth between the mill and parking lot. The overgrown path between the building and cracked-cement rectangle that was located close to the road was hardly safe given their circumstances, and the distance between Harper and Zander felt daunting despite the bright sunshine and warm breeze.

"I spent an hour doing your hair this morning," Zander reminded her, his eyes flashing as he pressed his back against a tree. His knees ached from his position, crouching low to the ground to keep out of sight, but he'd rather risk sore joints than an errant ghost elbow – or something worse – marring his perfect features. Unlike Harper, he couldn't see ghosts. That didn't mean he couldn't recognize the fuss their invisible friend was kicking up or the inherent danger associated with their current predicament. "I'm going to be really angry if you mess it up and I have to fix it."

Harper made an exaggerated face. She was used to Zander's whims, but even she had limits. Since they were in the middle of a day that started with an argument in bed, moved on to a snit over oatmeal, and then ran smack dab into an angry mill worker who died fifty years before and didn't want to leave his earthly resting place, she'd crossed that limit at least twenty minutes ago.

"You're the one who insisted on doing my hair," she started.

Zander offered her a derisive snort. "That is not how I remember it. I believe your exact words were 'Zander, I'm in trouble with Jared and I need to look really good for our lunch date so he forgets he's irritated with me.' Because I'm a good friend, I took pity on you and now you look beautiful."

Harper narrowed her sea-blue eyes. "Are you saying I don't look beautiful without your help?"

Zander knew enough about women to realize he'd stepped in it, but that didn't stop him from blowing past her evil expression. "You're always beautiful, Harp. I knew it first, in case you've forgotten. I told you in kindergarten that you were beautiful."

"Um, you told me in kindergarten that I looked like Supergirl when I tied a towel around my neck and pretended I could fly."

"It's the same thing," Zander said, unruffled. "If you picked Wonder Woman instead I would've upgraded that to most beautiful woman in the world."

"Why is Wonder Woman better?"

"She has better accessories and boots. Plus, well, I love you dearly, Harp, but your shoulders aren't broad enough to make people believe you have super human strength."

Harper had no idea how he did it, but somehow she felt insulted. "My shoulders are fine!"

"They're fine for a bustier. They're not fine for a full leotard. Also, well, you're kind of flat-chested. You can't pull off a big emblem like Supergirl. Wonder Woman doesn't have that problem."

Now Harper was convinced that she'd been doubly insulted. "I am not flat-chested!"

"You're not without curves, don't get me wrong, but you're hardly on par with the Kardashians."

Harper made a disgusted face. "I'm taking that as a compliment."

"I have so much to teach you," Zander lamented, sighing before he ducked his head to avoid a rock that slammed against the tree trunk right next to his ear. "Leonard Gibbons is not handling this well, by the way. When are you going to help him move to the other side?"

Leonard Gibbons was a 1950s mill foreman who accidentally fell into the moving wheel during a sudden spring storm. How? That was one of those urban legends that had different answers depending on who was asking the question.

According to the Whisper Cove Historical Society, which consisted of Delta Dobson and a microfiche machine, Leonard lost his footing thanks to a huge gust of wind and he fell through one of the upper doors and landed on the wheel, dying instantaneously. Given Leonard's anger, Harper didn't believe that for a second.

According to other gossip, which basically consisted of Doris Martin repeating what her mother told her one drunken night twenty years before, one of Leonard's workers was having an affair with his wife. The worker shoved Leonard through the second-story door … and then proceeded to marry his wife. Whisper Cove's public records showed that Barbara Ray Gibbons had married suspiciously fast after becoming a widow, but no formal charges were ever brought.

Either way, Harper didn't have a lot of options. As co-owner of Ghost Hunters, Inc., she'd been hired to do a job. The old mill, which sat vacant for decades, was due to be torn down in less than a week. A new outdoor market would be erected in its spot and Leonard's propensity for haunting – which included purposely tripping people and trying to drown them in the nearby river – had to end before construction crews descended.

That's why Harper and Zander were there. Their job was to help displaced spirits cross over. They'd been doing it for years and had built up quite the reputation. Most of that reputation was even good, their nonstop banter notwithstanding.

"Leonard is a real douche," Harper said, carefully pushing a strand of her shoulder-length blond hair behind her ear. "I guess we know why someone pushed him."

"You can't say that," Zander argued. "He might've been perfectly fine in life. Perhaps a harsh death is what turned him into a douche. You don't know."

"I guess that's fair," Harper conceded. "He's definitely a douche now, though."

"Oh, definitely." Zander glanced over his shoulder to scan the uneven path leading to the mill. He hadn't even made it inside before Leonard attacked. It was as if he knew what Zander and Harper were there to attempt. "How do you want to handle this?"

"Well, I was thinking I would run in your direction and when Leonard chases after me you can toss out the dreamcatcher. Easy peasy."

"I can't believe you just said 'easy peasy,'" Zander grumbled, annoyed. "If I didn't know better I would think you were drunk or something."

Harper balked. "Lots of people use that expression."

"No one I would ever be seen in public with," Zander countered, tilting his head to the side as Leonard began to wail. "We need to do something. The longer we stay and do nothing, the more riled up he gets."

"And the more riled up he gets, the more at risk my hair becomes."

"I knew it!" Zander extended a finger. "You are worried about your hair. Admit it."

Harper heaved out a sigh. "Fine. I admit it. I'm having lunch with Jared. After this morning, I want to look pretty."

Zander's expression softened. "You always look pretty, Harp. Jared knows that. He's not really angry about this morning."

"He seemed angry."

"I think he just likes acting tough," Zander offered. "He's kind of like one of the thugs in *Grease*. It's all about posturing. He's really a marshmallow in a tough guy's clothing."

Harper pursed her lips as she considered the statement. "That's an interesting way of looking at it. I can't wait to tell Jared your theory on his inner marshmallow."

"Please do," Zander said, bobbing his head. "So ... are you ready to end this?"

Harper's smile slipped into a grimace. "As ready as I'll ever be."

"Then let's do it. Just make sure you watch your hair."

"I'm on it."

FOR A man who spent the night with a beautiful woman, you sure seem surly."

Mel Kelsey's eyes were keen as they skimmed over his partner shortly before noon. He was used to Jared Monroe being happy-go-lucky and pleasant. The expression on the handsome man's face was anything but pleasant today.

"I'm not surly," Jared said, refusing to move his eyes from his computer screen. "I'm merely concentrating."

"On what?"

"Work."

"What work?" Mel asked, genuinely curious. "The only action we've seen in the past four days is that group of kids who accidentally bought oregano instead of pot and spray-painted the dealer's car with a monkey as payback, and Tammy Garner, who almost got hit by a car because she was jaywalking."

"It was a pirate."

"No, I'm pretty sure she was almost hit by a car."

"Not that," Jared said, his eyes flashing as he finally met his partner's gaze. "The kids didn't paint a monkey on the car. It was a pirate."

"Are you sure?" Mel wasn't convinced. "It looked like a monkey to me. Those ears were … huge."

"Those were earrings."

"But why would they paint a pirate?"

"Why would they paint a monkey?"

Mel tilted his head to the side, considering. "Good point. Moving along. Do you want to tell me what's bothering you? You've been one step short of singing as you kick your heels together for the past two weeks. I haven't seen you so much as frown in that time. Why are you so crabby today?"

"I'm not crabby," Jared replied, shaking his head. "I'm simply … tired. I'm so, so tired."

"Is Harper keeping you up at night? If so, I don't want to hear about it. I've known her since she was a child. She'll always be a child to me, for the record. That's what I think when I see you together. It's inappropriate and gross."

"Thanks for the update. Harper is not the problem, though," Jared said, rubbing the back of his short-cropped hair as he made a disgusted face. "Her roommate, on the other hand, is another story."

"Ah." Mel fought the urge to laugh as he regarded the hangdog expression on Jared's face. The younger police officer was a recent transplant to Whisper Cove, which was located along Lake St. Clair in Southeastern Michigan. Since Jared hadn't grown up in Whisper Cove, he wasn't familiar with the extreme lengths of Zander's larger-than-life personality. It was something that took some getting used to. "What has my nephew done this time?"

Mel was a man who loved his family. He considered family loyalty to be more important than almost anything else, in fact. That didn't mean he was oblivious to Zander's grating personality.

"He crawled into bed with Harper this morning," Jared replied, his eyes darkening.

"If you're worried about them hooking up, you should probably let it go," Mel said mildly. "They've been best friends since the day they met. Zander doesn't roll that way."

"I know that." Jared made a "well, duh" face and let loose with a low growl. "I'm not an idiot. I'm not worried about them hooking up."

"Then what's your problem?"

"I was in bed with Harper."

"Oh." Mel smirked. "Well, that had to be uncomfortable. He didn't … I don't know … try to hold your hand or anything, did he?"

"No, he was on the other side of Harper," Jared replied, annoyed. How could Mel not be getting this? "We were naked, though. We were up late last night and we were naked this morning. Do you understand what I'm saying?"

Mel rolled his eyes so hard Jared was momentarily worried he would topple over if he wasn't careful. "Did you have to tell me that?"

Now it was Jared's turn to hide his smirk. "What do you think I'm doing over there every night? Do you think we're holding hands and watching *Little House on the Prairie* episodes?"

"Oh, don't ever watch those with Zander around," Mel intoned. "He gets offended by the fashion. The girls wore the same dresses for four seasons and he was convinced it was some sort of prairie conspiracy."

Jared's mouth dropped open. "I … what?"

"It doesn't matter," Mel said, waving off Jared's incredulity. "As for this morning, well, have you considered telling Zander how you feel? Maybe if you explain about the nudity … ."

"He knew about the nudity. The walls are paper thin in that place."

"Oh, this conversation is taking a really uncomfortable turn," Mel said, his cheeks burning as he shifted his eyes away from Jared. For some reason he suddenly couldn't focus on the man without considering the fact that he might be a sexual deviant. In his eyes Harper was still a precocious child dragging around a stuffed dog as she spun fantastical stories about imaginary friends.

"Zander and I have talked about him entering the bedroom without knocking so many times I've lost count," Jared explained. "He nods and pretends he understands. Then he promises not to do it again. That lasts exactly three days and then he does it again."

Mel pursed his lips, amused. He'd always gotten a kick out of his nephew. The boy had stage presence. He noticed it at a young age. Zander couldn't help himself from being a pain. He very rarely set out to agitate someone – although it wasn't out of the question if Zander got a bee up his butt.

"I don't know what to tell you," Mel said after a beat. "What does Harper say about this?"

"Harper says she'll talk to him and apologizes for his actions. Then she distracts me with kisses … and by rubbing her nose against my cheek … and by making this little sighing noise that drives me crazy because it means that she's happy."

Mel barked out a laugh. "Oh, that's cute," he said. "You don't want to pick a fight because you're worried about making Harper unhappy. That's so sweet it makes me want to puke."

"It's not that."

Mel quirked a dubious eyebrow.

"Okay, it's not *just* that," Jared clarified. "I want her happy. I love it when she smiles. Zander doesn't bother me most of the time. The only time I want to kill him is right before we go to sleep and right after we wake up. If he could just learn some boundaries … ."

"You have to remember that Zander and Harper never had boundaries before you came along," Mel pointed out. "They never needed them."

"Well, I'm sick of feeling like the odd man out," Jared said. "Zander and Harper can't live together forever. This … threesome … cannot keep going on exactly as it's going on. Something has got to give."

Mel studied Jared's face for a moment, his expression unreadable. "If I were you, I would calm myself before saying anything of the sort to Harper. You're … um … not considering giving her an ultimatum or anything, are you?"

"That's not really my style."

"That's good. Women don't like that."

Jared knit his eyebrows together. "Why? Do you think she would pick Zander over me?"

"I think … ." Mel didn't get a chance to finish his statement because the sound of the front door opening jerked his attention in that direction. Jared followed suit, widening his eyes when he caught sight of an elderly woman who was so tiny she looked as if she could fit inside the huge purse she carried.

"Hello, Annette," Mel said, adopting an amiable tone. "How are you today?"

"I've been better." Annette practically grunted out her response. She looked as angry as Jared this afternoon. Mel could only hope it was for a different reason.

"What can we do for you?" Jared asked, pasting on a friendly smile. He'd never met the woman before so he was genuinely curious about the new face.

"Well … I'm pretty sure someone might be dead. There's a decent shot my late husband is the one who did the killing, too. It's basically been a real pisser of a day."

And just like that Jared's day tilted.

TWO

"Why don't you take a seat, Annette."

Mel was flabbergasted by the woman's announcement. He'd known her for as long as he could remember. She was considered "old" when he was a teenager. People called her "Old Lady Fleming" because she enjoyed calling the police and reporting rabble-rousers even back then. She was what his mother affectionately referred to as "a pill." Mel could think of a few other words to describe her, but now didn't seem like the time to dust them off.

"Can I get you something to drink?" Jared asked, his blue eyes filled with kindness. "We have coffee ... or water ... or tea. Which would you prefer?"

"I would prefer a fifth of bourbon. Do you have that?" Annette's face was full of annoyance as she planted herself in the chair across from Jared's desk.

"We don't have bourbon, Annette," Mel supplied. "I'm sorry."

"Why not? I would think with all the crap you deal with that bourbon would be a necessity."

"It's generally frowned upon to get loaded during work hours," Mel explained. "We tend to leave the bourbon drinking for when our shifts end."

"That seems like a stupid way to solve a crime, but whatever." Annette made a face that Jared would've found hilarious under different circumstances. However, he forced himself to remain somber given the reason for her visit.

"So ... that's no on the coffee, water, or tea?" Jared asked.

Annette heaved out a heavy sigh. "I guess I'll have some tea. I'll probably be up all night because of the caffeine, but it's not exactly as if beggars can be choosers. I need something to wet my whistle and bourbon is apparently off the table."

Jared pressed his lips together as he shuffled across the room and filled a mug with tap water before popping it in the microwave. He rummaged through the cupboard until he found the box of tea bags and plopped one in the steaming water before returning to Annette's side.

"It's Earl Grey," Jared said. "I hope that's okay."

"Nothing is okay without bourbon. I thought we already covered that."

Jared shifted his eyes to Mel, flummoxed. "I'm ... sorry."

Mel lifted his hand to placate Jared and shifted his attention to Annette. For her part, the woman – who couldn't have topped five feet even in stacked heels – sat stiff on the edge of her seat, the large purse (which could double as a suitcase for the right person) perched on her lap. "So, Annette, do you want to tell me what's going on here? You mentioned something about a murder."

"Oh, right," Annette said, slipping her hand inside the purse. "So, as you're both aware, my husband Arthur passed away recently."

"Yes, I was sorry to hear that," Mel said. "I went to his funeral. It was a lovely service."

Jared nodded his agreement even though he had no idea who Arthur was. He was fairly certain Harper and Zander attended the funeral, though, so he wasn't completely in the dark regarding the situation.

"It was a funeral," Annette scoffed. "There's nothing lovely about a funeral."

"Well, I just meant that people said so many great things about Arthur," Mel offered. "It was nice to hear all of the old stories and everything. He was beloved."

"Yes, I love a funeral where people lie, too," Annette said, disdain practically dripping from her tongue. "We all know Arthur was a big putz. If there was a poop stain in the underwear of life, it would've been Arthur. He was grouchy and mean … and a little racist."

Jared bit the inside of his cheek to keep from laughing. This was easily the most surreal conversation he'd participated in the last few weeks.

"Well, I guess we all remember him in our own special way," Mel gritted out, seemingly unsure of himself. "I'm not sure what his death has to do with a murder, though. If you're thinking someone went after him, I can assure you that the medical examiner found concrete proof that Arthur died of a heart attack in his sleep."

"I don't think Arthur was murdered," Annette said, wrinkling her nose. She had so many wrinkles on her face it was hard to differentiate where one started and another ended. "I'm surprised the medical examiner actually managed to find a heart in the first place. That's not why I'm here."

"So … why are you here?" Jared prodded. The more he talked to the woman, the more he couldn't help but like her. She was mean and short-tempered, but she had a certain pizzazz. He could imagine Zander turning out just like her in sixty years.

"I'm here for these." Annette removed a stack of old Polaroid photos, the edges yellowed from age, and handed them to Jared.

Jared wordlessly took them, frowning when his gaze landed on the first one and he recognized a woman's foot sticking out of a garbage bag.

"What is it?" Mel asked, easily reading the stiff set of his partner's shoulders. "Is it something kinky?"

"I'm not sure," Jared replied, riffling through the photos. Each subsequent photo made his stomach queasier. When he was done he handed them to Mel. "Do you know who that woman is, Mrs. Fleming?"

"I have no idea," Annette answered. "I couldn't rightly see a face. I'm getting old, though, so I was hoping you could see one."

"I saw a few profile pictures, but the face wasn't clear," Jared said, licking his lips. "She's clearly dead, though."

"I think the blood would be a dead giveaway on that one," Mel agreed, tilting a photo so he could stare at it. "These photos look pretty old, Annette. Where did you find them?"

"After Arthur died I decided to go up to the attic to sort through some things," Annette explained. "I thought it would give me something to do. Now that Arthur isn't around demanding I wait on him, I find I have a lot of time to burn."

"You shouldn't go up to that attic on your own," Mel chided. "You have an older home. Those steps are narrow."

"I'm old. I'm not dead." Annette's eyes flashed. "Last time I checked, I'm allowed to do whatever I want. I am an adult, after all."

"Forgive me for insulting you," Mel said, shaking his head as he returned his attention to the photos. "Where were they in the attic?"

"There's an old armoire up there," Annette replied. "I didn't even remember it being up there, quite frankly. It was from my former mother-in-law's house. You remember Gertrude, right? She was meaner than Arthur. She was uglier, too. He was no prize, but she was kind of like the pimple on the butt of the prize."

Jared made a big show of covering his mouth with his hand as he scratched his lip. Smiling now would be completely inappropriate. "Do you think the photos are left over from your mother-in-law's day?"

Annette shrugged. "I have no idea. I just saw a dead woman and figured I should make my problem your problem. I don't know who she is. I don't know how she died. I certainly don't know when she died."

"We can't be sure that this wasn't an accidental death," Mel cautioned. "There's blood but no murder weapon or anything. We'll have to do some investigating to figure out what's going on."

"I'm pretty sure that's why I brought the photos to you," Annette shot back, blithe. "I'm not an investigator. Despite your lack of bourbon, you supposedly are."

"Well, we'll definitely look into it," Mel said, exchanging a weighted look with Jared. "We might need to get into your attic. You know, just to be thorough."

"I figured as much," Annette said, struggling to her feet. "I'll get some garbage bags so you guys can sort through stuff while you're up there. It will save me some time."

Jared opened his mouth to argue with the woman. He wanted to tell her that cleaning her attic wasn't his job. Mel sent him a furtive headshake in warning, though, and Jared wisely snapped his mouth shut.

"We'll be in touch," Mel said. "Right now, I'm not sure what to think about any of this. We'll get to the bottom of it, though. I promise you that."

JARED was flustered by the time he reached the beachside restaurant. He was running late – and texted Harper to let her know that – but he prided himself on punctuality. He hoped she hadn't been alone at the table for too long. That didn't look to be the case when he found her sitting on the deck, though. In fact, she wasn't alone at all. She had a guest.

"I see you finally made it." Jason Thurman, Harper's high school boyfriend and the owner of the restaurant, slowly got to his feet and relinquished the chair he sat in moments before. "I kept your girlfriend company so she wouldn't feel abandoned and alone. I hope you don't mind."

Jared didn't bother to hide his scowl as he dropped a quick kiss on Harper's mouth and sat across from her. In truth, he liked Jason despite the fact that the man hit on Harper several times upon his return to Whisper Cove a few weeks before. He knew Jason was trying to get under his skin – and doing an admirable job – but he refused to let the restaurant owner know it.

"I don't mind at all," Jared said, adopting a friendly smile. "I was worried about Harper sitting here alone. At least now I know she wasn't lonely."

"She definitely wasn't lonely," Jason acknowledged, his eyes gleaming with mischief.

"Just bored," Jared supplied, pretending he didn't notice the way Harper rolled her eyes. She was used to the two men posturing. She'd grown to ignore it ... or at least pretend to ignore it. Jared was fairly certain she and Zander had a good laugh about every interaction once he was out of the room. "How was your day, Heart?"

Harper smiled at the nickname. Jared wanted something to call her that Zander didn't utilize. He came up with the moniker himself, and even though it made her feel girly and silly, Harper adored it. "Eventful."

Jared arched an eyebrow. "Do I even want to know what that means?" He was well aware of Harper's ability – being able to see and talk to ghosts was initially a strain on their relationship, but his disbelief was quickly squashed – but that didn't mean he was happy about her walking into continual danger. "You're not hurt, are you?"

"I am perfectly fine," Harper replied, grinning. "I didn't even get dirty. Doesn't my hair look fabulous, by the way?"

Jared didn't have the heart to tell her that he saw nothing different about her hair. "It looks great. I love what you did with it."

Harper narrowed her eyes, suspicious. "What's different about it?"

Crap. Jared had no idea how to answer. "It's … shinier."

Harper made a disgusted face. "It's wavy. Zander did it for me after you left this morning."

"Oh, well, at least he did something constructive today," Jared muttered, reaching for the menu. "It looks nice. I wasn't lying about that. It always looks nice."

"I asked him to do it because I knew you were angry about what he did this morning."

Jason's eyes lit up. "Oh, what did Zander do now? Is he crowding your little party of two?"

Jared scorched him with a murderous look. "Don't you have something to do?"

"Not really."

"Well, great," Jared grumbled. "For the record, no one is crowding our twosome. Our twosome is just fine."

"Is it?" Harper couldn't help but be a little worried. "You kind of stormed out this morning. I'm sorry about what happened, by the way. I've told Zander that climbing into bed with us isn't allowed. He just forgets sometimes."

Jason barked out a laugh, delighted. "He got into bed with you? How … cozy."

"We were naked," Harper explained. "I don't even notice it, but Jared gets self-conscious."

Despite his determination to aggravate Jared, Jason couldn't help but frown. "I'm sorry but … you were naked?"

"Don't even bother imagining it," Jared warned. "The reality is better than the fantasy and you'll never know what the reality looks like."

"Oh, that's so sweet," Harper said, patting his hand. "It's a little territorial, but it's sweet."

"I don't blame Jared for being uncomfortable," Jason offered. "I'm not sure how I would feel about it if that happened to me. Zander doesn't like lift the covers and look at stuff, does he?"

Harper was horrified. "Of course not!"

"He just climbs in and tells us about his date the previous evening … or whatever crap he watched on Netflix while we were sleeping … or whatever epiphany he had during a dream. It's mostly harmless. Er, well, except for the nudity."

The corners of Jason's mouth tipped up. "You're a better man than me. I wouldn't be able to put up with that."

"Well, I'm not sure how much more of it I'm going to be able to take."

"That's good," Jason teased. "That will give me a little time to wrap my head around the situation so I can swoop in and romance the crap out of Harper once you've hit your limit."

"And that's not going to happen," Jared said. Harper didn't realize she was holding her breath until he said the words. "I'm simply going to put a new lock on the door and make sure he can't get in."

"Oh, well, that sounds like a very pragmatic idea," Jason deadpanned. "I'm sure a flimsy bedroom door lock will keep Zander out. That sounds highly probable … or not."

"Ignore him," Harper said, grabbing Jared's hand as he glowered at Jason. "He's just trying to get to you."

"He's doing a good job of it."

"I'm … sorry."

The expression on Harper's face was so heartfelt it caused Jared's stomach to clench. "It's not your fault, Heart. We'll figure it out. If I have to beat up Zander or hide all of that expensive night cream he uses, we'll come up with a solution."

"Are you sure?"

"I'm sure."

"Okay." Harper blew out a relieved sigh and then decided to change the subject. "So why were you late?"

"Um, do you know Annette Fleming?"

"Old Lady Fleming?" Jason looked sick to his stomach. "Is she still alive? Does she still chase kids with a broom on Halloween? Does she still try to hit small dogs when she's driving down the road?"

"I have no idea about any of that," Jared replied. "She came in today with photos of a dead body, though. She says she found them in her attic. She thinks either her husband killed someone or her in-laws did away with a woman and then stuck her with the photos. The in-laws owned the armoire where the photos were found."

"I don't really remember her in-laws," Harper mused. "Arthur was actually meaner than Annette, though."

"Yes, I find that difficult to believe." Jared dug in his back pocket and returned with a Polaroid snapshot. "I probably shouldn't show you this, but I'm hoping you recognize something. We don't even know who the victim is … or when she died."

Harper sucked in a breath when she took the photo, her heart rolling. "Oh, my."

"Nice lunch gift," Jason intoned.

Jared ignored him. "I don't suppose you recognize her, do you?"

"I don't know," Harper replied, rubbing her cheek. "I don't recognize her, but I feel as if I should. Does that make sense?"

"Not particularly, but I'm hoping you'll go to Annette's house to look around with me after lunch," Jared replied. "If there's someone or something hanging around the house … ." He didn't say it out loud, but he was mildly hopeful Harper would stumble across a ghost to answer their questions.

"I understand," Harper said, mustering a small smile. "If I do this, though, do you promise to forgive me for this morning?"

"For the naked incident or the blueberry oatmeal snafu?"

"Both."

Jared held his hands palms up and smiled. "There's nothing to forgive."

"Then I'll go with you."

The duo lapsed into comfortable silence as they perused their menus. Jason was the first to break it.

"Okay," he said, intrigued. "I have to know what the blueberry oatmeal snafu is?"

"No, you don't," Jared and Harper answered in unison.

"Trust me, dude," Jared added. "You're better off not knowing."

Jason wasn't convinced, but he let it go. "I'll grab some soup for you guys as a starter. I'll be back to take your order in a few minutes."

THREE

"What do you think we'll find?"

Harper was antsy as she sat in the passenger seat of Jared's department cruiser, her hands busily bouncing around as she stared out the window. She didn't know why, but she was nervous. The photographs were disturbing on their own merit, but she couldn't shake the feeling that things were about to shift further … and in a truly terrible way.

"I don't know," Jared answered, his eyes thoughtful as they landed on her. "You seem … off."

"I'm fine." Harper's voice was unnaturally high and she internally cursed herself for not taking a moment before uttering the lie. Sure, it was a little white one and not a flaming whopper. It was still an obvious falsehood, though.

"Yes, you sound fine," Jared said, his lips quirking. "You're fine and dandy, right?"

Harper sucked in a steadying breath. "Okay, if I tell you something, do you promise not to laugh?"

"No."

Harper frowned. "No?"

"You say some genuinely funny things, Heart," Jared pointed out. "I think you could be a sitcom actress if this whole ghost thing fizzles out. Of course, you're far too hot to be on a sitcom." His eyes lit with mirth as she made an exaggerated face. "I promise not to laugh. Tell me."

"Now I don't know if I should tell you," Harper grumbled, crossing her arms over her chest. "I'm feeling vulnerable."

Jared sobered. "I'm sorry. I didn't mean to hurt your feelings. I promise I won't laugh. This is a serious situation ... even though we have no idea what we're even dealing with yet. This could be a murder or it could be something else entirely."

"Like what?"

"Oh, I'm not falling for that," Jared chided. "Tell me what you're thinking. When we're done with that, we'll talk about my weird theories."

"Okay." Harper ran her tongue over her teeth and squared her shoulders. "I have a feeling that we're about to see something terrible."

"Like what?"

"I have no idea. It's just this feeling of dread sitting in the pit of my stomach. It's been growing for the past hour. It's worse than the time Zander told me that *Children of the Corn* was miscategorized at the library and it really belonged in the non-fiction section."

Jared barked out a laugh. "He may be irritating, but he's kind of funny sometimes, too."

Harper's sea-blue eyes flicked to Jared, uncertainty lining her mouth. "Speaking of that, if you're angry and really serious about not being able to put up with much more ... um ... ."

Jared cut off Harper by grabbing her hand and squeezing it. "I shouldn't have said that. I wasn't being serious. I was playing macho for Jason. It wasn't fair to you and I'm sorry."

"It's obviously wearing on you," Harper pointed out. "I don't want you to be upset."

"Harper, I'm not upset. I'm agitated – that's for sure – but I'm not mad at you."

"I'll talk to Zander again," Harper promised. "I'll make sure he understands."

"He *does* understand," Jared argued. "He knows exactly what he's doing. He just enjoys doing it."

"It's not that," Harper protested. "He's just used to having me all to himself. We spent years only having each other to rely on. A lot of people think that makes us co-dependent."

"I happen to be one of those people. That doesn't mean I don't like him. I often have a great time watching your friendship play out because you guys are laugh-out-loud funny. We still need some privacy."

"I know." Harper looked caught, her eyebrows knitting together as she chewed on her bottom lip. "Maybe I'll make a deal with him that all of our bedroom activities have to be done in his room from here on out."

Jared was intrigued. "That sounds mildly dirty, but I think I know what you're saying."

"I would get up a few days a week and go into his room so we can gossip and bond."

"I think that sounds more than fair for everyone involved," Jared offered. "I like Zander. He makes me laugh and we have a great time together. I just don't like him climbing into bed with us. It drives me crazy."

"Is it the nudity?"

"It's everything," Jared replied. "That's our quiet time. I'm not asking you to pick me over Zander – I never would – but I don't think a little bit of privacy is too much to ask for."

"It's definitely not," Harper said, holding Jared's hand between both of hers. "He'll understand."

"I hope so."

"If he doesn't, you should definitely pick up that lock you were talking about, though."

Jared snickered. "You've got it." Jared narrowed his eyes as he turned onto a narrow driveway. It wasn't paved, sparse gravel creating an uneven path instead. It was also exceedingly long. "This is the house, right?"

"This is it," Harper confirmed, releasing his hand and leaning forward so she could study the sagging Victorian. "I've always wanted to see inside of this house."

"You've never been inside?"

"Annette isn't known for being friendly. She doesn't invite people over, especially if she thinks you were a delinquent as a child."

"Oh, my little delinquent," Jared teased, rubbing his hand over the back of her head. "I'm guessing that means she wasn't fond of you and Zander during your formative years, huh?"

"As far as I can tell she's never been fond of anyone, and that includes her husband."

"Oh, she made that perfectly clear," Jared said. "I can't understand why she married him if she hated him so much."

"She probably didn't have a lot of options. Back in the day, if you were twenty and unmarried you were considered a spinster. Marrying a bad guy was probably preferable to that."

"Ah, the good old days," Jared teased.

"Meh. I prefer having time to date and get to know someone. I'm enjoying it immensely, in fact."

Jared grinned. "Me, too. Now, come on. Let's see if we can find a ghost. Wow. There's a sentence I never thought I would hear myself say."

Harper giggled. "I'll bet you never envisioned yourself doing that during the good old days, huh?"

"Nope. I wouldn't change it for anything, though."

"THIS IS what I imagine the inside of Zander's brain to look like."

Harper was flabbergasted several minutes later as she stood in Annette's attic and surveyed the overflowing abundance of long since forgotten items.

"He's your poofy friend, right?" Annette's expression was unreadable as she glanced at Harper.

"That's not nice." Harper wagged a finger. She was a guest in Annette's home, but she had no intention of putting up with the senior citizen's guff. "Zander is a human being. He's a good man."

"I didn't say he wasn't. I just mentioned that he was a poof. That's not an insult." Annette's tone was dry and she seemed unbothered by Harper's irritation.

"That's totally an insult."

"Is not."

"Is, too."

"Is not."

"Is, too."

"Hey, Cop, was that an insult?"

It took Jared a moment to realize Annette was talking to him. "My name is Jared."

"I'll never remember that," Annette said. "It's a weird name. I don't understand why people can't pick normal names for their kids. Jared sounds like something you store pickles in."

Harper bit her lip to keep from laughing as Jared plastered an even smile on his face.

"Cop is fine," he said after a beat. "What was your question?"

"Is calling blondie's poofy friend a poof an insult?"

Jared didn't hesitate when he answered. "Yes."

"Oh, whatever," Annette muttered, rolling her eyes. "Do you know what this world's problem is? Sensitive people. We didn't have sensitive people when I was growing up."

"Yes, I'm sure you were too busy walking forty miles one way in foot-high snowdrifts to get to school," Harper said, feigning sweetness.

"You've got that right," Annette said, bobbing her head. "As for the photos, I found them over there." She lifted her hand and extended a gnarled finger. "They were in the drawer on the bottom there."

"The wardrobe?" Harper moved in that direction, being sure to tread lightly so she didn't accidentally trip over the multitude of boxes and bags of clothing. "You should really get someone to come up here and go through all of this stuff. It's probably not sanitary to leave it up here like this."

"That's what he's going to do," Annette said, jerking her thumb in Jared's direction. "He's going to clean the attic while searching for clues."

"That's not technically in my job description," Jared said dryly.

"You'll live." Annette made a face as she shifted from one foot to the other. "Unless you need anything else I'm going to head downstairs and put my feet up."

"Oh, of course," Jared said, his expression conflicted. "Do you need me to help you downstairs?"

"I need you to be quiet when you're searching for stuff," Annette shot back. "My story is about to start and I don't like noise when I'm watching it."

"Your story?"

"Her soap opera," Harper supplied.

"Oh." Jared forced a smile. "Well, I hope you find a lot of love in the afternoon."

Annette's face twisted into an expression that had Harper sucking in her laughter. "If I were you, blondie, I would be worried about this one being a poof, too. Perhaps you attract them. I saw a woman on a television show once and she said that was her special gift. She called it a curse, though."

"I'll ... keep that in mind." Harper's face remained frozen until she was sure Annette was out of earshot and then she dissolved into giggles. "You're sure you're not playing for Zander's team, right? Now I'm legitimately worried I attract a certain type of man."

"You're not funny," Jared said, shaking his head as he glanced around the attic. "This place is a complete and total mess. It's going to take hours to go through everything. If she wants us to pack it up we'll die of old age up here."

"Well, have fun with that," Harper teased, reaching for the handle of the wardrobe.

"Wait!" Jared's voice was so loud Harper jolted. "You need to put on gloves. This is technically a criminal investigation."

"Oh, right." Harper waited for Jared to hand her two latex gloves and then wrinkled her nose as she slipped them on. "Don't ever tell Zander about this. He'll have fashion nightmares for weeks."

"I'll try to refrain," Jared said dryly, taking Harper by surprise as he pressed a quick kiss to her forehead. "Thank you for helping me, by the way. I'm not sure I said that before. You were a good sport with Mrs. Fleming. You could've gone off on her and I appreciate the fact that you held your tongue."

"She doesn't mean to be insulting."

Jared cocked a dubious eyebrow. "Are you sure about that?"

"Well, no," Harper conceded. "I just meant that she doesn't do it out of a place of malice. She honestly doesn't think there's anything wrong with her attitude. It's kind of refreshing in a weird way."

"I think Zander is going to be exactly like her at that age."

Harper tilted her head to the side, considering. "Wow. That is a terrifying thought."

"Do you think I'm wrong?"

"I think it's really good you're getting that lock."

Jared barked out a laugh as he moved away from Harper and knelt next to an antique chest on the floor. The hinges were tarnished, but after a few minutes he managed to open the lid. It was filled to the brim with old clothing and costume jewelry.

"Why would anyone keep this stuff?"

Harper shrugged as she turned her attention back to the wardrobe. "Some people are simply packrats. They can't seem to help themselves."

"You're not a hoarder, are you?"

"I have a few things I have sentimental attachment to, but I'm not a hoarder or anything," Harper answered. "Zander, on the other hand, has hoarder tendencies. He has a storage bin at that place on the east side of town and he stopped letting me look inside three years ago. I'm not taking that as a good sign."

"What do you think he has in there?"

"I have no idea. I'm afraid to look."

"Well, as long as he's not filling your house with unnecessary stuff and collecting dryer lint or anything, I guess it doesn't matter."

Jared and Harper spent the next hour working in comfortable silence. They occasionally called attention to a random item, but everything they stumbled across was neither nefarious nor mildly suspect. They filled eight garbage bags with items to be tossed before Harper moved to the window to take a breather.

It was hot in the attic, the Victorian without air conditioning. The air was stale and stifling when Harper finally decided to open the window. She struggled with the aged frame, trying three times before she finally forced it to give way. The air outside wasn't much cooler given the doldrums of summer, but Harper sucked in gasping mouthfuls of fresh air as she dropped to her knees.

"I thought I was going to pass out there for a second."

Jared, his brow slick with sweat, widened his eyes. "Why didn't you say something?"

"Because I didn't want to seem like a wuss. This is official business, after all."

"Yeah, but you're officially more important to me than business," Jared countered, pressing his hand to her forehead and frowning. "You're very warm. Stick your face through the window."

"You're kind of bossy," Harper grumbled, but she did as instructed, resting her head against the sill as she studied the heavy trees behind the lot. "This house must be worth a fortune."

"Do you really think so?" Jared couldn't help but be surprised. "It's practically falling down."

"Victorians have a lot of charm," Harper supplied. "They're a lot of work, don't get me wrong, and I think they're only practical if you have a lot of children. I wasn't just talking about the house, though. The house would clearly need a lot of work."

"What were you talking about?"

"The location," Harper replied, her eyes skimming the trees. "The river is only about five hundred feet beyond the tree line, too. If I owned this parcel I would clear a path between the house and river."

"And put a hammock at the river? You know how I love hammocking."

Harper grinned at the joke. She'd introduced Jared to the joys of a hammock shortly after they started dating. Now he was obsessed with spending lazy weekend days swinging in the breeze. "A hammock would be a must."

Jared groaned a bit as he got comfortable on the floor next to Harper, his knees cracking. "Would you really want a house this big? I'm going to be honest, Heart, I like a smaller house. I like a home that feels cozy."

"I like a Victorian in theory but not practice," Harper replied. "I wouldn't want to clean this place. It has three floors not counting the attic, too. That's not practical when you're older."

"It doesn't seem to bother Annette."

"That's because she was a tank in another life."

Jared snickered. "That's pretty funny. Okay, I say we take a five-minute break and get back to it. If the break involves kissing, so much the better. What do you think?"

When Harper didn't immediately answer, Jared shifted his eyes to her and found her gaze intent. She stared at a specific spot in the middle of the thick trees, seemingly oblivious to everything but the one focal point, and gripped the windowsill so tightly her knuckles turned white.

"What is it?" Jared asked, his voice barely a whisper.

"There's a ghost out there. I thought I was seeing things at first … but she's there."

"Do you know who it is?"

Harper shook her head. "I just see a white dress and brown hair."

"Kind of like the photo, huh?" Jared exhaled heavily. "I guess that means all of those alternate theories I came up with probably aren't going to fit the facts at hand, huh?"

"That would be my guess," Harper said, finally dragging her gaze from the woods to Jared. "We need to go down there. I think she wants to show me something."

"That's why I brought you," Jared said, linking his fingers with hers. "Lead the way. If she leads us to a body, though, we're going to have to come up with a plausible reason for being in the woods."

"We'll cross that bridge when we come to it. Come on."

FOUR

"What's going on?"

Annette was alert as she watched Harper and Jared traipse through her house. Instead of heading for the front door – which they entered through – the couple pointed themselves toward the back, drawing Annette's attention away from the television where a sexy man with limited acting ability was in the middle of ripping off his shirt.

"We need to check something outside," Jared replied, mustering a smile for Annette's benefit even as he kept one eye on Harper. His blonde seemed to be focused on her task and he didn't want to risk her disappearing into the woods when he wasn't around to lend her backup. "We'll head back upstairs in a few minutes. We need a little air."

Annette briefly narrowed her eyes and Jared got the distinct impression that she wanted to challenge him on the story but ultimately she shrugged and turned back to the television. "Be quiet when you come in. The mobster dude is about to do it with the blonde and I want to see if he knocks her up. He has super sperm or something."

"Super sperm?"

"He has like eight kids and he doesn't look as if he showers. Something has to be super about him."

"Okay," Jared said, shaking his head. "We won't be gone long."

By the time he focused on the back door, Jared realized it was open and Harper had already stepped through it. He raced after her, sucking in a breath when he found her standing on the back lawn staring at a large pine tree.

"What do you see, Heart?"

"It's a woman."

"The woman from the photos?"

"I couldn't really see the woman in the photos," Harper replied. "The ghost has the same color hair, though."

"And the same color dress," Jared murmured, linking his fingers with Harper's and following her toward the woods. "Heart, do me a favor and stick close. Don't go running off into the woods, okay?"

"The woods aren't very big. It's not as if I'll get lost."

"I want you close to me," Jared said. "It's important."

"I ... why?" Harper was genuinely curious.

"Because if there's a body around here I need to make sure you don't step on any evidence."

"Oh." Harper couldn't help but be mildly disappointed. She thought for sure he would say something romantic. It was silly, but she'd gotten used to his sultry conversational skills.

"I also would never get over it if something happened to you and I want to be there to protect you in case the ghost gets rowdy," Jared added.

"That was much better."

"I know." Jared dropped a kiss on the tip of her nose and then moved beyond the tree line, his eyes wary. "Do you still see her?"

"She's walking," Harper replied, lifting her hand. "That way."

"Okay, we'll take it slow," Jared said. "You lead the way, but be careful."

"I'm always careful."

"Be more careful than that."

Jared kept firm hold of Harper's hand as they trudged through the trees. It was a warm day, but the pine trees were so close – and tall – that it felt cool beneath the thick boughs. Even though they were outside, Jared couldn't help but feel a little penned in. It was an odd feeling.

"These trees are old," he murmured.

"Yeah. This entire area was pretty rural up until like forty years ago," Harper explained. "Even then it didn't become a tourist destination until about twenty years ago. We're only fifty minutes from Detroit, but it still feels like a lifetime because the big city hasn't managed to touch us yet."

"I like the small-town atmosphere."

"I do, too," Harper said, a hint of a smile tugging at the corner of her lips. "I hope the big city stays away from Whisper Cove forever."

"That would be nice, huh?"

Something occurred to Harper and she kept her eyes on the ghost, who kept popping in and out of existence as she weaved through the trees, and worked overtime to keep her voice neutral. "I thought you wanted to move to a bigger police market at some point."

"I haven't ruled that out," Jared said. He knew exactly what bothered Harper, but he wasn't keen on a big discussion when they were following a ghost through the woods. "Even if I move to a bigger market, that's not going to change our relationship, though. I'll still be close. You said it yourself. Detroit is fifty minutes away. I can commute if it becomes necessary."

"Right." Harper tugged on Jared's hand and led him around a wide pine tree, the ghost floating over a small hill before disappearing.

"Harper, I haven't decided if I still want to go to a bigger market," Jared said, opting to tackle the problem head-on instead of letting it fester. "We've talked about this. I'm happy here. I'm not looking to leave anytime soon."

"Won't you feel that I'm holding you back?"

Jared shook his head at her earnest expression. "No. Every time I look at you all I can think about is moving forward."

"Oh, that was so sweet." A wide smile split Harper's face. "So sweet."

"This isn't my first romantic walk in the woods," Jared teased, tugging her close for a moment so he could wrap his arms around her. "It's going to be okay. Whatever happens, we'll figure it out together."

"Good."

"I might even let Zander have a vote."

Harper giggled as she pressed a kiss to his cheek and took a step back. "I'm sorry to bring our relationship drama into an official situation. That wasn't right."

"It's just us. I don't mind. If you did it in front of someone else I might have a problem with it. We're alone, though. It's okay."

"We're not quite alone," Harper said, her eyes landing on the ghost as she stood next to a fallen tree close to a fence. "We have a friend."

"What is she doing now?" Jared asked, following Harper's gaze. He couldn't see the ghost, but he liked to

imagine he could so Harper didn't always feel so alone
with her ability.

"She's standing by that tree." Harper pointed and
Jared released her hand so he could move closer. Harper
maintained eye contact with the ghost and remained several
steps behind Jared. She didn't want to tread on his turf if it
wasn't necessary. "Do you have a name?"

Harper was talking to the ghost, but Jared couldn't
stop himself from making a lame joke. "It's Jared. I answer
to 'cop,' though."

Harper ignored him. "Do you know who you are?
Do you have any idea why you're here? Is your body out
here?"

The ethereal woman didn't answer, but she pointed
to a spot about two feet in front of Jared. She looked sad …
and a little confused.

"She's pointing right in front of you," Harper
offered, glancing to her right. "The river is right over there.
I didn't realize it was so close. It's slow moving in this
area."

"I didn't even hear it," Jared muttered, squinting as
he dropped to one knee and gently shoved a mounded pile
of pine needles out of the way. "Oh, well, crud."

"What did you find?" Harper dragged her eyes from
the river and took a step closer. She sucked in a breath
when she realized what Jared was looking at. "Is that a …
hand?"

"Yeah."

"The bones look old."

"This body has definitely been here for years,"
Jared said, digging in his pocket. "I need to call Mel and
get the medical examiner out here. You did it again, Heart.
You're amazing."

Harper knew he meant it as a compliment and smiled accordingly, but she couldn't stop her stomach from turning as she focused on the ghost. The woman looked forlorn and lost. Harper felt anything but amazing as she looked at her. *Now what?*

"OKAY, WE'VE got a female in her late thirties … maybe early forties … and she's been dead for at least twenty years."

John Farber, Macomb County's chief medical examiner, removed his gloves with a loud snap four hours later. He looked tired but mildly intrigued.

"Can you tell me anything else?" Jared asked.

"We're going to have to do some work and it's not going to be easy," Farber replied. "The skull is intact for the most part, although a section appears to be missing. That could indicate a head wound, but the bones are so brittle from being exposed to the elements for an extended period of time – and we have no flesh to deal with – that we can't immediately determine a cause of death."

"Could it have been accidental?" Harper asked. She was unnaturally pale and Jared didn't miss the fact that her hand kept fluttering to her stomach. He'd been so engrossed watching Farber work that he lost track of his blonde for a bit. She disappeared from the examination room for a long period of time and he didn't think anything of it. Now, looking at her drawn features, he couldn't help but wonder if she felt ill.

"I guess it could've been accidental," Farber replied. "Someone clearly buried her, though. I think the proximity to the river is what caused the body to be discovered. I guess it's good you guys decided to take a break from the attic to get some air and walk by the river, huh?"

"We got lucky," Jared agreed, keeping his gaze level. It hadn't been difficult to decide on a lie to include with the official report. "It was stifling in that attic and I was worried Harper might pass out."

Harper scowled, her eyes flashing. "I wasn't going to pass out."

"It's okay. There's no harm in it." Jared's gaze was pointed. He didn't want Farber looking too closely at their actions. "If someone buried her, though, how did her hand end up above the dirt? She didn't try to climb out, did she?"

"Are you asking if she was buried alive?" Farber asked, chuckling. He was young for a medical examiner – in his mid-thirties – and his eyes sparkled as they skimmed Harper's slim body. "She wasn't buried alive. We've had wet springs several times over the past four years. That area showed signs of regular flooding from the river. The hand emerged due to simple erosion."

"Well, that's a relief," Jared said. "How long will it take you to find a cause of death?"

Farber shrugged. "It's not exactly going to be a walk in the park. It's going to take some time. I … hold on. I need to get that." Farber glared at the phone on the wall as it incessantly dinged and strode toward it, leaving Harper and Jared alone.

"Are you okay?" Jared brushed his knuckles against Harper's cheek.

"I'm fine." Harper said the words but averted her gaze.

"You're pale, Heart. You look … queasy. Are you sick?"

Harper heaved out a sigh. "It's this place. I've never been to a medical examiner's office before. I don't know what I was expecting. This isn't it, though."

Jared glanced around, confused. "It's a normal lab."

"It's so ... sterile."

"It has to be that way."

"I know. It's just sad."

Jared ran his tongue over his teeth as he slipped his arms around her waist, tugging her close and kissing her cheek as he rocked back and forth. "Have you seen something?" he whispered, smiling as Farber locked gazes with him.

"There's no ghost here, if that's what you mean," Harper replied, keeping her voice low. "I feel sadness, though. I feel loss. This place is heavy. Can't you feel that? I feel as if something is sitting on my shoulders and my stomach feels shaky."

"I think you're probably super sensitive to this stuff because of who you are and what you can do," Jared countered. "I should've taken that into consideration. I should've dropped you at home ... or the office ... instead of bringing you with me. That wasn't fair."

"You couldn't have known. I didn't know. Why should you?"

"I don't know, but I still feel guilty," Jared murmured, brushing his lips against her cheek. "I'll get you out of here the second Farber is off the phone. There's no reason to stay."

"I don't want to rush you."

"You're not rushing me." Jared cupped the back of her head as he pulled back to stare into the fathomless depths of her eyes. "Farber can't give us more information right this second. It's not as if this is a pressing issue. This woman has been dead for at least twenty years. Even if the killer is still around, he doesn't seem to be an immediate threat."

"How do you know it's a man?"

"Just a hunch." Jared gave Harper another hug as Farber returned to stand in front of them. "Do you have anything else that would be of interest that I can chase tonight?"

"Not right this second," Farber replied, his expression unreadable. "Just for the record, though, you're the first partners I've had in here who've reacted to a murder by hugging one another."

"We're not partners," Jared replied. "She's my girlfriend."

"Do you take your girlfriend to crime scenes often?"

"More often than you might think," Jared answered, slipping his arm around Harper's waist and directing her toward the door. "Harper isn't feeling well. It's not every day that you take a walk in the woods and stumble across a body. We're going to get out of here. You have my email. Fire off your initial report as soon as possible."

"I'm on it," Farber said, his eyes twinkling. "Just for the record, though, I would be willing to console Harper for a little longer if you have something else to do."

Jared scorched Farber with a narrow-eyed look. "I'll handle the consoling."

"I don't need consoling," Harper interjected. "My stomach is just a little upset."

"Well, I make a mean pot of chicken noodle soup, too," Farber offered. "It's my mother's recipe. It's guaranteed to cure whatever ails you."

"All that ails me is a long day," Harper said, mustering a smile. "Don't worry about me. I'll be fine."

"She will," Jared agreed. "I'll make sure of it."

Farber held his hands palms up and grinned, remaining rooted to his spot as he watched Harper and Jared walk toward the door. The blonde really did look ill as she rested her head against her boyfriend's shoulder.

"We'll stop at the store," Jared suggested. "I'll cook dinner for you."

"That sounds nice. Are you just doing it because you think he was hitting on me, though?"

Jared was affronted. "Do you think that's the kind of guy I am?"

Harper answered without hesitation. "Yes."

"Well, you're right," Jared said, causing her to giggle. "What is it with you and men? Do you cause every guy who comes into contact with you to fall all over himself or what?"

"Just the lucky ones."

"I guess I'm glad to be one of the lucky ones," Jared said, holding open the door. "Now I'm going to have to make you soup to prove I'm the better man, though."

"Oh, fun. I'm looking forward to that."

"You might not say that if you end up with food poisoning. You'd better hope I pick a good recipe from the internet."

"I guess we'll have to wait and see how things turn out, huh?"

"That sounds like a plan."

FÍVE

"How about some juice?"

Jared felt like a mother hen with all of the clucking he was doing as he meandered around the local grocery store with Harper. She remained pale, which worried him, and she seemed almost disconnected from their conversation.

"What?" Harper dragged her eyes to Jared and he jolted when he saw how washed out they were. On a normal day he felt as if he was looking into a vast ocean. Now he felt as if he was looking into a tiny puddle.

"Heart, maybe we should take you to the clinic," Jared suggested, moving his hand to her forehead. "You're a little warm."

"I'm fine. Don't worry."

"I can't help but worry," Jared countered. "You look downright exhausted. I know spending time with me can be tiresome, but you're taking it to an absurd level." Jared offered her a wink to let her know he was kidding, but Harper didn't bother to grace him with a smile for his efforts.

"I'm fine."

"Yeah, that makes me know you're not," Jared said, grabbing a jug of orange juice from the shelf and dropping it in the cart. "Under normal circumstances you would've given me a kiss and flirted, maybe given me a preview of what you had planned for tonight. If you're too tired to do that, I know something is wrong."

"I'm fine." Harper had said the words so many times since leaving the medical examiner's office that even she knew they were lacking. "You don't have to worry. I promise. I'm … okay."

Jared didn't believe her for a second. "You're not okay," he argued. "You're a little warm. You're definitely pale. You're also quiet. Those three things grouped together are enough to worry me. Do you know what happens when I get worried? I get sick. Do you want us both to be sick at the same time? I'm thinking that would be a miserable experience."

Despite her irritation, Harper couldn't help but smile. "That actually kind of sounds like it could be fun," she said, her eyes lighting up with the first bit of life Jared managed to glimpse there in hours. "We could spend the day in bed and eat soup together. We could watch soap operas and make Zander wait on us. Ooh, we could make him use a fake accent when he delivers tea."

Jared chuckled, smoothing her hair as he studied her angular features. "That does sound fun in a demented sort of way. The problem is, knowing Zander, he'll want to climb into bed with us and drink the tea. Then he'll get sick, too."

"Oh, no." Harper firmly shook her head. "That's the one time Zander wouldn't touch my bed … even if he was in a plastic bubble with his own oxygen supply. He's deathly afraid of germs."

"Oh, well, that's good to know," Jared said. "I'm going to get an empty bottle and write 'Ebola' on it and leave it out. That might solve our problem. I'll spray him with a fake bottle of Ebola water – like a cat – whenever he climbs into bed with us."

Harper giggled, the sound warming Jared's heart. She still looked weary and wan, but it was a step in the right direction.

"You're funny," Harper said. "You always know how to make me feel better."

Jared sobered long enough to tilt her chin back so he could trace the dark circles under her eyes. "I don't think I've done my job well enough today. I was thinking we could get the ingredients for soup so I can wow you as a cook and make you forget about the medical examiner and then we could go to bed early and watch television or something."

"Ah, an exciting night in Whisper Cove."

Jared smirked. "I'm fine with a quiet night in Whisper Cove. In fact, it sounds just about perfect right now. Whenever we get an exciting night that often ends with you running from a killer while I think I'm going to have a heart attack."

"A quiet night sounds nice," Harper conceded. "You don't have to make soup, though. I don't care about Farber."

"Are you sure? He probably makes double the money I do."

"I don't care about money."

"He seemed interested in you," Jared pointed out. "He thought you were cute. I kept catching him staring. I wanted to punch him in the nuts to get him to look away. That's frowned upon in police circles, though."

Harper's peal of laughter was so cute Jared couldn't help but grin. "I don't care about Farber," she repeated. "He may have more money, but you have a much better personality."

Jared scowled. "That's what people say right before they preface it with 'it's not you, it's me.' I don't want to have a good personality."

"You're also ten times hotter," Harper offered.

"Oh, well, that sounds totally better," Jared said, puffing out his chest. "Scratch everything I said before. Being hotter is the best way to go."

Harper didn't have to fake a smile as she grabbed a bag of shredded hash browns to cook for breakfast the next morning. After adding a dozen eggs, she moved around the aisle's endcap and froze in her place.

"We need some bacon, too," Jared said, oblivious to the shift in her mood. "Bacon will make us both feel better. In fact, maybe we can make bacon soup. I ... oomph." Jared slammed into Harper, quickly extending his hands and holding her shoulders so she wouldn't accidentally pitch forward. "What the ... ?"

Harper's mouth was open as she stared at the frozen food aisle, her blues eyes wide and bewildered. Her hands gripped the handle of the cart so forcefully that her knuckles turned white.

"What the heck are you doing, Harper?" Jared asked, annoyed. "You're supposed to keep the flow going. That's proper market etiquette."

Harper didn't immediately answer. Instead she grabbed Jared's arm and jerked him in the direction of their previous aisle. She remembered to bring the cart as an afterthought ... but just barely.

"Do you want to explain what you're doing?" Jared asked, confused. "Has your illness suddenly made you crazy? If so, we need to get you to the clinic. I'm not messing around here."

"Didn't you see that?" Harper hissed.

"See what? All I saw was the back of your head when my jaw crashed into it."

"That." Harper pointed in the direction of the frozen food aisle.

"I can't see through the aisles, Heart," Jared said, working overtime to tamp down his irritation. "I'm hot and sexy. I'm not superhuman, though."

"We'll have to agree to disagree on that," Harper shot back. "There have been plenty of times where I thought you were superhuman."

"Oh, that's cute," Jared said, tucking a strand of hair behind her ear. "Just wait until you realize I can cook soup, too."

"Focus!" Harper barked out the word and caused Jared to jolt. "I need you to be very stealthy and poke your head into that aisle without being obvious. Tell me what you see."

"Is this some sort of elaborate prank?" Jared asked dryly. "If you make me look in that direction and run in the other direction so I have to chase you, we're going to have words."

Harper made a disgusted face and pointed. "Go."

"Good grief." Jared cast three suspicious glances over his shoulder to reassure himself that Harper remained where he left her as he shuffled toward the adjacent aisle. He finally gave his full attention to the frozen food section – even though he remained convinced this was some sort of joke at his expense – and when he did he pulled up short.

At the end of the aisle – at the intersection of frozen pizza and Lean Cuisine – Zander stood with another man. They were intent on each other, not even bothering to glance at the other shoppers. At one point the man with Zander, who had blond hair and blue eyes, tilted his head back and offered a loud guffaw. Zander put his hand on the man's arm and joined in the laughter. Jared was so caught up in the scene he jerked his head to the side when he felt Harper slip into the place next to him.

"It's Zander," Jared offered dumbly.

"I know." Harper looked morose. "Did you see the guy with him?"

"I did."

"Do you think they were on a date?"

"Who cares?" Jared asked, recovering. "If he's on a date, great for him. If not, that doesn't solve our immediate problem. Where did we land on the bacon soup?"

Harper's expression was murderous as she leveled a dark gaze on him. "I can't believe this is happening."

"I THINK you should put out an Amber Alert."

Harper paced her kitchen an hour later as Jared studied the recipe card and added ingredients to the huge pot on the stove. She'd been a distracted mess since leaving the grocery store. She wasn't exactly known for being levelheaded on the best of days, but Jared couldn't be certain that she wasn't experiencing some sort of mental incident.

"You want me to put out an Amber Alert on Zander?" Jared asked, tipping the cutting board so the carrots and celery slid into the pot. "Amber Alerts are for children."

Harper made a disgusted face. "Zander is like a child. That's why he's always irritating you."

"Yes, I'm well aware of that," Jared said. He refused to be dragged into an argument when he had no idea why he was supposed to be upset. "He's technically an adult, though. Amber Alerts are also for individuals who have been kidnapped."

"You don't know Zander hasn't been kidnapped," Harper pointed out. "He could've been sending out secret signals to the people around him. We weren't close enough to tell."

"Uh-huh." Jared handed the container with the chicken bouillon to Harper. "Open four of those cube things for me, will you?"

Harper's mouth dropped open. "Excuse me?"

"I'm listening to your rant," Jared assured her. "I just thought you could help with the soup while you're doing it."

"Oh, I see what you're doing," Harper muttered, opening the container and grabbing a foil-covered cube. "You're trying to make me feel as if I'm acting crazy even though I know I'm the only one acting sane."

"I would never insinuate you're acting crazy," Jared countered, mouthing the word "wow" to himself when he knew she wasn't looking. "I think you're acting completely sane. In fact, I think you might be underplaying it. Zander's on a date. Surely the end of the world is right around the corner. Except … er, well … Zander has a date every other night."

"Do you think it was a date?" Harper blinked rapidly, causing Jared to sigh.

"Is that a trick question?" Jared couldn't help but be flummoxed.

"That wasn't a date," Harper said, shaking her head. "They probably met at the gym or something. Zander adores telling people about his magic berry protein shakes and he gets the ingredients from the frozen food section."

"That must be it," Jared said dryly, planting a lid on top of the pot before shifting his eyes to the clock on the wall. "Forty-five minutes until I add the noodles. I have to tell you, Heart. I'm pretty proud of myself. I just made chicken noodle soup from scratch."

Harper stared blankly at Jared. "If Zander was just showing that guy how to make a proper shake, where is he?"

Jared knit his eyebrows together, annoyance warring with confusion. "Harper, I don't understand why you're freaking out. Zander has dates all of the time. You encourage him to date. Heck, I want him to date more. If he could finally find someone he could put up with for more than a night – you know, someone without hairy toes or an outie bellybutton because those are travesties of nature that he obviously can't look past – then maybe he would occasionally be interested in staying in his own bed."

Harper was horrified. "You're enjoying this."

Jared was at his limit. "This? I'm not enjoying this at all. I enjoyed having lunch with you today. I enjoyed working with you. I even enjoyed part of our shopping trip even though I worried you were getting sick. I'm not enjoying this, though."

Instead of reacting with anger, Harper chewed on her bottom lip as tears burned her eyes. "I'm sorry."

"Oh, geez." Jared took a determined step toward her and rested his hands on her shoulders. "What's wrong with you, Heart? I am seriously going to take you to the clinic right this second if you don't come up with a rational explanation for the way you're acting. I think you might've suffered a stroke or something at the medical examiner's office."

"I didn't have a stroke!" Harper exploded, her eyes filled with fury. "I'm worried about Zander."

"You're not worried. You're mad."

"I ... am mad." Harper blinked furiously as tears threatened to fall. "I'm mad. Oh, I'm mad and it's not fair. What's wrong with me?"

"Don't even think about crying," Jared warned, wagging a finger as he pulled her in for a hug. "You need to tell me what's going on here, Harper. I feel as if I accidentally stepped into an alternate universe or something. Is this an episode of *Star Trek* and nobody told me?"

"It's Zander."

"I figured that out myself," Jared said, stroking the back of Harper's head. "What's wrong?"

"He didn't tell me."

Jared stilled. "He didn't tell you what?"

"That he was dating someone."

She was opening up and yet Jared remained confused. "Harper, he dates a different someone every other day."

"And he texts me details on each one," Harper said, her eyes filled with sorrow. "He didn't text me about this one. He didn't tell me about this one."

"So? I'm sure it was an oversight."

"It's not an oversight," Harper snapped, jerking away from Jared. "We always tell each other everything about the people we're dating. Do you know that after I met you we didn't have a discussion that didn't revolve around you for days?"

Jared couldn't help but smile at the admission. "No, but we're definitely going back to that later. I'm dying to hear what you said about me."

"I said you were stubborn and full of yourself and Zander said that meant I liked you and to suck it up because you probably had a few redeeming qualities to make up for the arrogance."

Jared's smile slipped. "Yes, well, it all worked out in the end," he said dryly, rolling his eyes. "Harper, I know you and Zander are incredibly tight, but you have no idea what's going on here. For all you know they did meet at the gym and then they decided to run to the grocery store together.

"They might not even have been on a date," he continued. "They might've just met in the store, for all we know. Give Zander time to tell you. Jumping to conclusions isn't going to help anyone. It's probably perfectly innocent."

Harper smoothed her shirt and tilted her head to the side as she considered the suggestion. "I guess you have a point."

"I definitely have a point," Jared said, snagging Harper around the waist and pulling her to his lap so they could get comfortable on one of the kitchen chairs. "It's going to be okay. Zander is probably going to come running through those doors any second and then we won't be able to shut him up."

Harper felt mildly silly about her meltdown as she rested her head against Jared's shoulders. "You're right. I'm acting like an idiot."

"Idiot is a strong word," Jared countered, kissing her cheek. "I am happy, however, that you seem to have shaken off whatever knocked you back at the medical examiner's office. I was definitely a bit worried about you there."

"I feel better," Harper said. "I'm sure I'll feel great once your soup is ready. Good job on that, by the way. I'm really impressed."

"Thank you!" Jared smacked a loud kiss against her lips. "I am the king of soup."

"Does that mean I'm your queen?" Harper teased, her eyes flashing.

"You can be whatever you want to be, Heart." Jared rubbed his nose against Harper's. "It's going to be okay. Everything is going to work out. I promise. I'm sure there is a rational explanation for all of this."

six

"Good morning."

Farber was all smiles as he ate his McDonald's breakfast sandwich next to the cleaned bones in the medical examiner's office the next morning.

"Good morning," Jared said, making a face. "How can you eat with those bones right there?"

"I'm hungry."

"Yes, but there's a dead body *right there*," Jared said, pointing. "I don't understand how you can possibly eat knowing that."

"You adjust to certain things when you're in this line of work," Farber supplied. "It's not a big deal. You just get used to it. When I was in medical school we used to eat Chinese food while doing full autopsies … and we're talking bodies with flesh and organs. This is just bones. It doesn't bother me in the slightest."

"Don't take this the wrong way, but you're a sick man."

Farber winked, amused. "How could I possibly take that the wrong way? Speaking of being a sick man, though, what's the deal with your girlfriend? Do you always take her on investigations?"

Jared shifted uncomfortably from one foot to the other, unsure how to answer the question. "I … what do you mean?"

"Your girlfriend, the hot blonde."

"I know who my girlfriend is," Jared said, scowling. "I also know she's hot. Just for the record, I made her soup last night and she was totally wowed by it. Thanks for the idea."

Farber wasn't bothered by Jared's tone and he let him know it by making an "o" with his mouth and fanning his face. "Oh, you put me in my place," he teased. "I guess since you made her soup that means I don't have a shot, huh?"

"You don't have a shot because we're happy," Jared clarified. "The soup only cemented that."

"For a man who is happy, you look a little worn down," Farber pointed out. "What's that about?"

"I *am* happy, so don't bother thinking otherwise," Jared warned, extending a finger. "I'm also tired because Harper was up all night. I didn't get any sleep."

"Ooh, sexy."

"It wasn't that," Jared said, rolling his eyes. "Trust me. If it was because of that I would be tired but smiling."

Farber's eyes filled with sympathy. "I'm just messing with you. Did she get sick? She looked a little shaky when you guys left. She's probably not used to seeing dead bodies. I get how that can throw people off."

"She was shaky until we hit the grocery store," Jared supplied. He had no idea why he was confiding in a man he barely knew. "I was really starting to get worried and then we saw Zander on a date. You would've thought the world was ending. She had a complete and total meltdown. It vanquished her sickness pretty darned quick."

"Who is Zander?"

"Her roommate."

Farber rubbed his cheek as he tilted his head to the side, considering. "Your girlfriend has a roommate?"

"It's a long story."

"She has a *male* roommate?"

"I just said it was a long story."

"Yes, well, I'm dying to hear it," Farber said. "That has to be quite the strain on your relationship."

"It's not so bad," Jared said, holding his hands palms up. "They're incredibly tight. It's no different than if she had a woman for a best friend. Sure, it's annoying when Zander climbs into bed with us in the morning, but I totally have a plan to nip that in the bud."

Farber's eyes widened to comical proportions. "So, wait, are you telling me that your girlfriend lives with another man, he crawls into bed with you and creates a really creepy threesome, and she's jealous because he goes out on dates and you're perfectly fine with it? No offense, man, but I would start looking for some testicles if I were you."

Jared's scowl was dark and pointed. "She's lived with Zander for a very long time and I have no intention of getting between them. There are no creepy threesomes. Zander likes to gossip over his morning coffee. It's actually fairly innocent. And, for the record, Harper is not jealous of Zander's date for the reasons you think."

"Ah, but she is jealous," Farber intoned. "I think you might be lying to yourself, my friend. I get it, don't get me wrong. That's a stunning woman. You're going to end up with a broken heart if you're not careful, though."

"Zander is gay." Jared had no idea why he felt the need to make the announcement. He wasn't keen on spreading around anyone's private information, and yet Farber's antagonistic tone put Jared on edge.

"Oh, that makes things better ... kind of," Farber said. "The roommate is gay so the threesome isn't kinky – although it still sounds a little kinky, just on your end now

– and the jealousy is not about romance. This is like a soap opera and yet I can't look away. Why is she jealous?"

"Because he didn't tell her about the date," Jared replied. "She had an absolute freakout because we saw them in the grocery store and Zander didn't tell her about the date before it happened. Then, he came in long after we went to bed. She was up and she wouldn't stop muttering."

"Was he alone when he came home?"

Jared nodded. "It's not about the sex … or whatever it is that they're doing. She's upset because he didn't tell her he was dating someone. That's totally not like him. On a normal date night he leaves to meet the guy at a restaurant and he's usually texting Harper because the date has a unibrow or mismatched highlights by the time the salad is served. He always finds something wrong with a date and very rarely goes on a second date."

"It sounds as if they're co-dependent."

"Oh, they're completely co-dependent," Jared said. "I'm used to that. This was … something else. Harper is usually easygoing and fun to be around. Last night she was like a different person."

"Oh, well, if you don't like that other person you can always pass her over to me," Farber suggested.

Jared made a growling sound in the back of his throat. "That's never going to happen," he said. "You push that idea out of your head right now."

Farber mock saluted. "Yes, sir."

Jared rolled his eyes so hard he worried he might momentarily lose his equilibrium. "Let's get back to business, shall we? What did you find on my victim?"

"Well, I have a name and some very minor background information," Farber supplied, balling up his breakfast sandwich wrapper and tossing it in the empty bag before shuffling closer to the bones. "Her name is Tess Hilliard and she disappeared twenty-five years ago."

"How did you match the identity so quickly?"

"Because Whisper Cove is so tiny that only four people have disappeared from the area without being found in the past thirty years."

"Oh, well, that would do it."

Farber smirked. "Hilliard had dental records on file. They're a match. I pulled up the missing person file on her and all it said was that she was forty at the time of her disappearance and that she had a reputation for sleeping around. The cops at the time posited that she took off with a guy and wasn't a victim of foul play."

"I guess they were off on that," Jared muttered, rubbing his chin. "There wasn't anything else in the file?"

"Not on our end," Farber replied. "You might have better luck, though. I believe the old physical files are still in the storage room at the department."

"And I guess that's my next stop," Jared said, flashing a smile. "Thanks for the information."

"I'll be in touch when I have a cause of death."

"Thanks for that, too," Jared said, stilling as he reached for the door. "As for the things I said about Harper, I didn't mean them. She was manic last night but that doesn't mean there's an opening for someone else."

"You know I'm just messing with you, right?" Farber asked. "I think she's pretty, but it's clear you two are devoted to each other. I'm stuck in this lab all day. I have to get my jollies somewhere."

"See, it's too bad you're not gay," Jared said. "You and Zander would love each other."

Farber's smile was charming. "Never say never."

"I'll be in touch," Jared said, shaking his head. "Thanks for everything."

AND THEN I was like 'there's no way I'm going to go out with you if you think women are only good for having babies and cleaning the kitchen.' He thought I was being bitchy and would feel better if I got pregnant. Can you believe that?"

Molly Harper, GHI's lone paid intern, perched on the corner of Harper's desk and recounted the previous night's dating extravaganza with gusto. The young woman, her short hair a violent shade of blue today, used her hands as she emoted.

"That sounds horrible," Harper said, licking her lips as she focused on Molly's face. She generally enjoyed the woman's company, but Harper had other things on her mind this particular morning. That didn't mean she couldn't at least feign interest. "What did he say?"

"He said that God created women to bear children and that we're going against his will if we don't do it," Molly replied. "He asked me if I liked being a sinner. I asked him if the mental hospital knew he escaped."

"It sounds to me as if he's on to something." Eric Tyler, GHI's technical guru, flashed a mischievous smile as he cleaned a camera lens. All four of the Ghost Hunter, Inc. employees were in the office at the same time this morning. That was a relatively odd occurrence. "I think you should definitely go for him, Molly. You might see your horizons expanded if you pop out a few kids and learn how to make a rump roast."

Harper bit the inside of her cheek to keep from laughing at the murderous look on Molly's face. The girl considered herself a feminist to the core – and she made sure everyone she came into contact with realized that, too – so she was naturally affronted by Eric's suggestion.

"I'm going to put my foot in your rump roast," Molly snarked, making a big show of kicking Eric's rear end as he moved past the desk. "Don't men understand how insulting that is to women?"

"I think that men only care about their own feelings and ignore women altogether unless they need something from them," Harper replied automatically, her eyes narrowing as they landed on Zander. For his part, her erstwhile best friend seemed to be oblivious as he worked on balancing the books across the way. He didn't even bother pretending to engage in the conversation.

"Wow," Molly intoned, her eyes widening to saucer proportions. "Did you and Jared have a fight?"

The question was enough to pique Zander's interest, but only marginally. "Oh, don't tell me Detective Whinebox is still giving you grief because I climbed into bed with you yesterday morning. If he is, I'll talk to him. It was a genuine accident. I forgot."

"Wait … you climbed into bed with them?" Eric was horrified, and oddly intrigued.

"I do it all of the time."

"But … they're dressed, though, right?"

"I don't care either way," Zander replied. "I've seen Harper naked so many times it's not even a curiosity anymore."

"Holy crap," Eric muttered, shaking his head. Up until a few weeks before he'd been harboring a one-sided crush on Harper. He'd moved on – er, well, mostly – but the mental image clearly set back his progress. "Wait, is Jared naked during these morning interludes, too?"

"He is, but it's not as if I look," Zander explained. "I already have the same equipment he does so there's no reason to stare. I mean, he has abnormally large nipples, but I've almost gotten over that."

Molly pursed her lips, amused. "Nipples?"

"Jared's nipples are normal," Harper said. "Don't listen to Zander. He's just … being Zander."

"Oh, we should make a television show called *Being Zander*," Eric suggested. "I'm sure that would be a huge hit on the Oxygen network or something."

"The Oxygen network?" Zander couldn't help but be affronted. "It's Lifetime or bust for me, baby. Don't insult me. The Oxygen network. Good grief."

Harper giggled at his mock outrage and then remembered she was angry with him. Zander's eyes locked with hers when he realized she'd stopped laughing and he didn't miss the conflict lurking in the shadow of her eyes.

"What's wrong, Harp? Uncle Mel said you and Jared found a body in the woods behind Annette Fleming's house yesterday. Was it terrible?"

"It was all bones," Harper replied, her tone cool. "There's a ghost out there, but she won't talk to me yet. I'm going to have to figure out a way to get through to her."

"Well, you'll do it," Zander said. "You always do."

"Yes, well, thank you." Harper's demeanor was unnaturally stiff, although she was pretty sure Molly was the only one picking up on her agitation. "We had to spend a few hours at the medical examiner's office yesterday afternoon and then I felt a little sick."

Zander's eyes flashed. "Because you saw dead bodies?"

"I'm not sure why," Harper admitted. She hadn't let herself dwell on that situation for very long after she caught sight of Zander and her entire evening was burned to ash. "Jared cooked homemade soup for me, though, and I felt much better after I ate."

"That's good," Zander said. "That Jared is a handy guy."

"He is," Harper agreed, an idea forming. "We went to the grocery store before heading home. We had a great time picking out items for the soup."

"You went to the grocery store?" Zander appeared surprised.

"We did," Harper confirmed, her tone heavy and pointed. "We totally did."

"Well, I'm glad Jared is such a good cook," Zander said, getting to his feet and averting his gaze. "You have good color in your cheeks and you're obviously feeling better. I have a few things to do this morning and then we have a job this afternoon. I'll meet you there."

Harper was flabbergasted. "Wait ... you're leaving?"

Zander refused to meet her intense gaze. "I'm running errands. I'll see you at the afternoon gig in a few hours. Molly, I think you did the right thing by shutting that guy down. He sounds like a real tool."

And with those words Zander flounced out the door, leaving Harper with something akin to heartburn as she rested her hands on the top of her desk.

"He was sure in a hurry," Eric said, oblivious as he grabbed two cameras. "That's not like him. He usually loves a good gossip session."

"He certainly does," Harper muttered under her breath as she stewed. "That definitely wasn't like him at all."

SEVEN

"So what's the background on this one?"

Eric unloaded his equipment from the back of Zander's car shortly before noon. He wasn't happy about the job being scheduled during their usual lunch hour, but he wisely kept his complaints to himself. He wasn't the most observant guy, but even he managed to pick up on the weird vibe between Harper and Zander as they drove toward the Markowitz farm.

"Janet Markowitz owns the farm," Harper explained, her eyes skimming the expansive parcel of land. The barn looked rundown and disheveled, the roof obviously sagging, but the rest of the property was in pristine condition. "It has belonged to her family since it was built – so over a hundred and twenty years. She inherited upon her father's death."

"Is he the ghost?"

"I'm not sure who the ghost is," Harper admitted. "Janet just called and said she didn't care what it would cost to catch a ghost and she would sign the contract when we arrived. She was even willing to pay a premium if we could do it right away. I told her we needed to scope things out and come up with a plan first."

"Well, that's always a bonus … when they want to give us a bonus, I mean," Molly said brightly. Her youth made her keen when it came to jobs. "Do you think I could be the primary on this one?"

Harper arched an eyebrow, surprised. "You want to be the primary?" She didn't miss Zander's firm headshake behind Molly's head. "I'm not sure you're ready for that."

"Oh, come on," Molly protested, annoyance flashing. "I've been watching you do it for almost a year now."

"That doesn't mean you're ready," Harper cautioned. She didn't want to dampen the young woman's enthusiasm but letting Molly run wild when they didn't know what they were dealing with sounded like a bad idea. "Let me get the lay of the land and then we'll talk about it."

Molly beamed. "Great!" She turned to help Eric collect his equipment and the moment she left Zander moved closer to Harper.

"That's a very bad idea," Zander murmured, keeping his voice low. "Our insurance isn't going to cover her if something bad happens."

Harper knew he had a point, but she was so agitated with his secret-keeping that she couldn't help but muster an argument – even though she knew it was altogether lame. "How do you know something bad is going to happen?"

"I don't but … ."

Harper didn't give him a chance to finish the sentence. "For all you know it could be a passive ghost, a friendly ghost even. I know it doesn't happen very often, but we've dealt with easy jobs before."

"Yes, but they're the exception rather than the rule," Zander pointed out, his nostrils flaring. That's how Harper knew she'd managed to truly agitate him. He didn't want to acknowledge the chill between them, but he refused to back down. "Are you saying you're willing to risk Molly's safety?"

Harper knew how to press Zander's buttons, but he was a master at making her want to yank out her hair. That's what happens when best friends work together. The fights aren't often but when they emerge they're almost always bad.

"Do you really think I'm saying that?" Harper challenged, frustrated.

Zander balked. "Of course not. I think you're letting Molly's enthusiasm cloud your brain, though. It's one of those feminist solidarity things."

Oh, now he was just purposely making things worse. Harper could think of no other explanation for Zander's insistence on digging his heels in. "Feminist solidarity thing?"

"You know what I'm talking about," Zander supplied. "It's like when you guys all group together to declare men evil for a day. You can't help yourselves. It's in your DNA or something."

Harper narrowed her eyes to dangerous blue slits. "I can't believe you just said that to me."

"And I can't believe you're fighting with me on this," Zander snapped. "Molly is not being primary. I'm co-owner of this company. My ruling stands."

Harper crossed her arms over her chest, defiant. "Really? I happen to be co-owner, too. Perhaps my ruling should stand."

"Don't push me, Harper!"

"Don't push me, Zander!"

"Hey, um, guys." Molly looked nervous as she shuffled closer to the duo. She'd obviously been listening, which meant Zander and Harper grew a lot louder than they initially envisioned. "There's an old lady walking this way and she doesn't look happy. I just thought you might want to know that before you start pulling out each other's hair or something."

"We're not going to pull each other's hair," Zander said, sucking in a breath as he took a step away from Harper. "I might, however, hide all of her fat pants so when PMS strikes this month she's going to have to go around naked."

"You suck," Harper muttered, shooting another hateful glare in Zander's direction before plastering a fake smile on her face and focusing on the woman closing the distance between them. "You must be Janet. I'm Harper Harlow. It's so nice to meet you."

The woman, who was dressed in overalls and flip-flops and wore a floppy straw hat on her head, didn't bother mustering a smile or shaking Harper's extended hand. "I am Janet Markowitz. You have a contract for me to sign, right?"

"I guess she's not in the mood to mess around," Eric muttered.

"We do," Zander confirmed, retrieving a sheet of paper from the bag at the back of the vehicle and handing it to Janet. "This basically says that you'll pay us for helping the ghost pass over and not go back on your word once the deed is done."

Janet snatched up the contract and looked it over, her eyes impassive as she scanned it. "This doesn't look very official."

Zander was good when it came to public relations, but he couldn't help but be offended. He spent weeks perfecting the optimal contract – even going so far as to buy special software to generate the documents – and he took it as a personal dig when someone didn't admire his work. "If you would like something else … ."

"It doesn't matter either way," Janet said, yanking an ink pen from the top pocket of the overalls and propping the contract against the side of the vehicle and signing with a flourish. "I just want this done."

"Well, great," Zander said, retrieving the contract. "I'll send your copy via email."

"I don't have no email. I've never seen any reasoning for doing it. People survived centuries before email."

Zander gritted his teeth but managed to appear calm. "Then I'll send it to you in the mail."

"Whatever," Janet said, waving her hand. "Just get rid of the ghost. It hops all over the property, but it spends most of its time in the barn."

"Did someone die there?" Harper asked, falling into step with the woman. "Was there a farming accident? Do you know how he died?"

"Oh, honey, it's not a he," Janet said. "It's a she. I've seen the dresses to prove it."

"Oh, well, that makes no difference," Harper said, reminding herself to remain placid as she conversed with the woman. Janet Markowitz had a way of getting under people's skin. That much was obvious. "Do you know how long the ghost has been here? Do you know who she is?"

"I know exactly who she is," Janet replied, unruffled. "She's my sister ... and I want her gone."

"HER SISTER?"

Even though they were fighting – or more aptly ignoring each other as much as possible as they pretended they weren't fighting – Zander couldn't help but voice his amazement a few minutes later as he walked toward the barn with Harper and Janet. Eric and Molly remained behind – there was no sense moving equipment if the ghost wasn't in the barn – so Zander and Harper were forced to handle Janet and her attitude alone. Thankfully for them, the woman appeared to be somewhat hard of hearing – or purposely ignoring them – and they could whisper amongst themselves as they made the trek.

"Yeah, that's definitely weird, right?" Harper lifted her eyes to the faced façade of the barn as they approached. "This thing looks as if it's one stiff breeze away from collapsing and killing us all."

"Which is why it would be a terrible idea to let Molly be the primary."

Harper let loose with a low growl. "Don't push me, Zander."

"If you two are done fighting, the door is right here," Janet said, her gaze pointed as she gestured to the gaping hole in the side of the barn. It didn't resemble a door in the slightest.

"This place is safe, right?" Harper couldn't help but be a tad dubious as she tentatively stepped inside. The light in the room was muted – only slivers of sunshine appearing through holes in the ceiling beams – and it had an unbelievably creepy vibe. "I think every horror movie ever filmed wishes it had this barn."

"You're a funny one, aren't you?" Janet asked, wrinkling her nose. "And when I say "funny" I mean queer and not full of giggle gumption."

Harper stilled, her eyes wide as she glanced in Zander's direction. "I'm sorry … queer?"

"She didn't mean it as an insult, Harp," Zander chided, shaking his head. "She just meant it as in odd. Isn't that right, Mrs. Markowitz?"

"I meant it as queer," Janet replied, unperturbed. "I have no idea what you guys are talking about."

Harper pressed her lips together, hoping it came across as a bemused smile and not an outright grimace. She maintained her cool quotient as she surveyed the barn, her eyes bouncing between various points of interest. "Tell me about your sister."

"What do you mean?"

"I think what Harper is asking is how do you know that the ghost is your sister? Have you seen a full-blown apparition?"

"I have no idea what you're asking," Janet grumbled. "I know it's my sister because she talks to me."

"She talks to you?" Harper couldn't help but be a little surprised. Even when people were aware of ghostly presences they couldn't hold full conversations with the unanchored spirits. The majority of hauntings were only detected because items moved … or a few random sounds tipped them off … or even a fleeting glimpse of a shadowy figure in a mirror. If Janet was having full conversations with her sister, that would be a first for Harper.

"Of course she talks to me," Janet barked. "Well, it's more like she bitches at me. You know what I mean, right? You guys are brother and sister and there's no one who can irritate you more than a sibling."

That was true. Harper and Zander weren't related by blood but that didn't mean they weren't brother and sister in their hearts.

"What does she do?" Zander asked, genuinely intrigued. "Does she say passive aggressive things instead of admitting she's angry because you hopped into bed with her boyfriend?"

Janet made a face that was downright comical. "How did you know about Stan? I never told anyone I slept with him."

Harper bit the inside of her cheek to keep from laughing. Even though Zander was making a point of picking a fight with her, he'd somehow stumbled on hilarious results. "Um, never mind about that," she said. "How did your sister die?"

"I don't know. I think she fell out of the loft or something."

Harper furrowed her brow, confused. "You don't know how your sister died? How come?"

"Because I'm old and I can't rightly remember," Janet replied. "Do you remember how everyone you've ever met died?"

"No, but if someone came back as a ghost I would surely remember that," Harper shot back, her patience wearing thin. "Only one person in my family came back as a ghost and I remember it very clearly." It had been her grandfather and she'd been crushed and confused when he appeared to her at such a young age.

"Well, bully for you," Janet intoned. "I can't really remember. I had eight siblings, for crying out loud. I can't possibly remember how all of them died – although I do remember Ronald. He got drunk one night and decided to tip a cow. It landed on him and he suffocated. His last words were … 'I'm a cow pancake instead of a pie.'"

Harper widened her eyes. "Is that true?"

"Of course it's not true," Janet scoffed. "The part about the cow is true. We weren't there when he died, though. If we were we would've helped him up, not listened to bad jokes."

"Oh." Harper risked a glance in Zander's direction and found his shoulders shaking with silent laughter. Part of her wanted to join in, but the other part remained angry. No, angry wasn't the right word. She was hurt. No, she was angry, too. She was angry *and* hurt. She was angurt. What? That was kind of a word.

"How long has your sister been dead?" Zander asked, directing the conversation to a safer topic.

"I don't know … like twenty years or so. Maybe it's been thirty. I can't rightly recall."

"And she's been haunting the barn ever since?" Harper was appalled.

"Yeah, she never had much of a life," Janet said. "She was always more caught up in her looks than anything else. She never understood that we had work to do and that's why she died. She wasn't paying attention because she didn't know that part of the railing in the loft was unsteady. If she'd bothered working that week, she would've realized it. It was the talk of the barn.

"Anyway, she put her hand on it and was yelling something stupid to me and she fell right over," she continued. "She made this big splat sound when she landed, too. The horses freaked out and tried to escape from the barn."

Harper's mouth dropped open as incredulity rolled over her. "I'm sorry. Is that true?"

Janet shrugged. "Mostly. My memory isn't what it used to be. It could've been more of a thud than a splat."

Zander opened his mouth to say something – although Harper had no idea what he could possibly add to this madness – but he didn't get a chance. Out of the corner of her eye, Harper noticed an old hay bale moving in the loft and she instinctively shoved Zander out of the way as it careened over the edge and landed on the spot he stood moments before.

"What the … ?" Zander instinctively hugged Harper close.

Janet was seemingly unbothered by the turn of events. "Yeah. That was Dorothy. Now you can see why no one liked her."

"Did she just try to kill me?" Zander sputtered, his face flushed.

"Why do you think the barn is in such bad shape?" Janet asked, annoyed. "So, when can you get her out of here?"

Harper rubbed her cheek as she stared at the loft. She hadn't caught sight of the apparition yet, but she had a clearer picture of what they were dealing with. "We need to put a stronger dreamcatcher together. I'm pretty sure your sister is a poltergeist, not a ghost."

"Is there a difference?"

"A big one."

Janet heaved out a long-suffering sigh. "Whatever. Just make it quick. I'm sick of the old bat and I want her gone. I've been more than patient, but enough is enough. You're going down, Dorothy. Do you hear me? You've had your last roll in the hay ... or roll of the hay, if you prefer."

Harper swallowed her distaste before responding. "Yeah. We'll get right on that."

EÍGHT

"What's going on with you and Zander?"

Molly wasn't one to mince words and after an uncomfortable (and mostly silent) drive back to the office she invited herself to accompany Harper on a walk around town. The blonde wasn't thrilled with the turn of events – she wanted to plot against Zander's tight lips on her own – but she couldn't bring herself to discourage Molly so she merely nodded when the intern offered her conversational services.

"Nothing is going on with Zander and me," Harper replied evasively, focusing on a kitschy storefront as they passed. "Why would you ask that?"

"Oh, I don't know," Molly deadpanned. "Perhaps it has something to do with the fact that you're barely talking. You guys usually talk about everything – including stupid stuff like what would happen if a race of spider aliens took over the world – so it's pretty obvious when you stop talking."

"Did Eric notice, too?"

"He's not a master of the obvious."

Harper heaved out a sigh as she dragged a hand through her hair. "It's nothing I really want to talk about," she said after a beat. "We're just having some issues."

"Because he climbs into bed with you and Jared so he can gossip? For the record, I find that unbelievably cute. I would love it if he did that to me. I think Zander is hilarious."

"Uh-huh."

"I can see why it bothers Jared, though," Molly plowed on. "Even a guy as sure of himself as Jared probably feels self-conscious being naked in front of another guy. It's probably not easy to refrain from comparing … um … hardware."

"Jared doesn't feel self-conscious," Harper clarified, pressing the heel of her hand to her forehead. "He has nothing to feel self-conscious about. Don't believe a word Zander says about his nipples. They're normal nipples."

"I wouldn't notice if they were large anyway," Molly said. "I would be too focused on his washboard abs and tight little butt."

Harper knit her eyebrows together. "How do you know about his butt?"

"You can just tell," Molly replied, unbothered. "He has that look about him."

"Well, I don't like talking out of turn, but his butt is truly phenomenal," Harper acknowledged, a rush of warmth washing over her when Molly giggled. "His abs are nice, too."

"And his nipples?"

"They're … manly."

Molly's giggle was so charming that Harper couldn't help but relax her stance. "He's a good man. He just wants us to have some privacy. Zander doesn't believe in boundaries. He doesn't think they apply to him."

"Have you talked to him about that?" Molly asked. "Is that why he's so … pouty?"

"I don't think what happened with Jared is making him pouty," Harper said, her mind flashing to the man she saw Zander laughing with in the grocery store the previous evening. "I think something else is going on."

"Oh, yeah? What?" If Molly noticed the way Harper's shoulders stiffened at the question she didn't let on. "I love Zander, but I'm betting he's a lot of work."

"You have no idea," Harper intoned as they rounded the corner, her mind busy as she tried to figure out a way to make Molly forget about her question. She hopped back when she realized she was about to careen into another person. It only took her a moment to shift from annoyed to happy, though, as Jared's face (and butt) swam into view. "Hey!"

"Hey, Heart. I was just coming to see you." Jared pulled Harper in for a long hug as he nodded in Molly's direction. "Hi, Molly. How are you today?"

Molly didn't bother hiding her wistful sigh. "I'm great. How are you?"

"I'm much better now that I got my fill of Harper," Jared said, his grin impish.

"Oh, I want one of you," Molly whined, making a face. "I think you're the only one of your species, though. I'm probably going to go through life alone … or having to fight of mouth breathers who think a woman's only purpose is cooking and childbearing."

"Do I even want to know what she's talking about?" Jared asked, shifting his eyes to Harper.

"Probably not," Harper replied, resting her hand on his chest for a moment, taking comfort in the soothing beat of his heart. "What are you doing here? You said you were coming to see me."

"I was hoping you were done with your job from earlier," Jared explained. "I have some information to share with you on the body we found yesterday and I was hoping we could talk over lunch. I'm starving."

"And here I thought you had your fill of soup last night," Harper teased. "Jared made homemade soup from scratch last night, Molly. It was delightful."

"Oh, now he's even cuter," Molly said, pursing her lips. "It's not fair. He has a great butt and washboard abs. He cooks. I don't care how freakishly large his nipples are. Nobody is perfect, but he's darned near close."

Jared's serene smile slipped at the words. "Zander?"

Harper shrugged. "You know he's fixated on your nipples. There's nothing I can do about it."

"I'm going to do something about it," Jared muttered. "I'm going to twist his nipples until they fall off. We'll see how he likes it."

"You boys will have to handle that on your own," Harper said. "I don't think I would be welcome in a nipple fight."

Jared wasn't sure that was the case, but he decided to let it slide. "I'll handle Zander. Don't worry about that. Did you talk to him about what happened last night? What did he say?"

Harper made an odd throat-clearing sound and shook her head to ward off Jared's line of questioning. She tried to be subtle, but her reaction was obvious to Molly.

"Wait, is something more going on than Zander climbing into bed with you guys?" Molly asked. "By the way, Jared, I would totally like to be the third wheel on that car if you ever want to branch out with other guests." She wiggled her eyebrows suggestively.

"I ... um ... thank you for the offer," Jared sputtered, his cheeks flooding with color. "I ... um ... ."

Harper sympathetically patted his chest as she attempted to swallow her smile. She wasn't completely successful. "Don't worry about it, sweetie. I would never allow that to happen. I'm fine with two guys. Two girls is a deal breaker."

Jared scowled as he shook his head. "I need to remember to buy that lock."

"That's probably a good idea." Harper glanced at Molly, unsure. "Um, Jared and I need to talk shop at lunch but … ."

"Oh, don't worry about me," Molly said, waving off Harper's concern. She knew the last thing her boss wanted to be was rude, but she had no intention of infringing on a romantic date. "I'll take care of my own lunch."

"Are you sure?" Harper was secretly relieved, but she hoped her face didn't betray that emotion.

"I'm totally sure," Molly said, grinning. "Just give his butt a good squeeze for me, okay?"

Harper couldn't stop herself from giggling. "You've got it."

Harper and Jared lapsed into silence as they watched Molly retrace her steps in the direction of the office. Jared made sure she was out of earshot before commenting.

"My butt?"

Harper affectionately patted his rear end. "It's very nice."

"But … ."

"It's a girl thing," Harper supplied. "Suffice it to say that you come out looking like a god at the end of the day, though."

"That's all I ask."

"SHOULD I even ask about your day or just plow into mine?" Jared asked once they were settled in the neighborhood diner and had placed their orders. "I want to be a good boyfriend, but you seemed weird when I brought up Zander earlier."

"That's only because I didn't want Molly to know what's going on," Harper replied. "She's well aware that Zander and I are ... off ... but she thinks it's because he climbs in bed with us."

"That's why I'm off."

Harper smirked. "He still hasn't mentioned his date, for the record. I even managed to bring up the fact that we were in the grocery store last night because I wanted to give him an opening. He didn't say a word about it. Instead he lied about having errands to run and took off."

Jared found himself on uneven footing as he sipped his water. He knew what he wanted to say, but he was anxious to avoid a fight. "I'm sure you guys will work it out," he said finally. "There still might be a perfectly good reason for him keeping this to himself."

Harper's eyes flashed. "And what reason would that be? He finds it necessary to involve himself in every aspect of our relationship and yet he lies about what he's doing. Why is that okay?"

"I didn't say it was okay," Jared clarified. "I merely said that it was ... there's no right answer to that question, is there?"

"Nope."

"Right. Moving along." Jared made an exaggerated face as he played with the straw wrapper next to his flatware. "Whatever you decide, I'm on your side. You can even tell Zander that when you fight ... and we both know you're going to fight."

"I'll keep that in mind," Harper said primly. "That's enough about me, though. Tell me about your day."

"Farber came up with an identity for the victim."

"That was fast."

"Apparently only four people have ever gone missing from Whisper Cove and never been found."

"And Quinn must be one of them," Harper mused, her eyes clouding briefly.

Jared mentally kicked himself for so casually mentioning that fact. Harper's previous boyfriend Quinn Jackson was involved in a car accident years before. His vehicle was found, including enough blood to make law enforcement officials believe he suffered catastrophic injuries, but he managed to wander away from the car before rescue crews discovered the vehicle. Either because of pain or blood loss, the man disappeared into the heavily wooded area surrounding Whisper Cove. His body was still out there.

"I'm sorry, Heart. I shouldn't have … ."

"Don't apologize," Harper said, waving off his concern. "You've done nothing to apologize for. It was merely a weird statistic."

"I'm still sorry." Jared gathered her hand and gave it a reassuring squeeze. "Anyway, her name was Tess Hilliard. She disappeared twenty-five years ago. She was forty at the time."

"Hmm." Harper rubbed her cheek as she ran the name through her head. "I don't really remember anyone by that name."

"You would've been a child when she disappeared," Jared reminded her. "Your parents probably didn't talk about it in front of you because it had no bearing on your life. According to Mel, she was known as something of a town … date."

Harper tilted her head to the side, confused. "Date? I don't know what that means."

"It means that she was popular with various men throughout the town," Jared replied. He was trying to be tactful, but it wasn't working out well. "Apparently it didn't matter if the men were older, younger, single or married. She dated them all."

"You're saying she was a slut."

"I'm saying that she was popular," Jared clarified. "We're trying to track down family members, but I was hoping to talk to people who knew Tess back in the day. Mel suggested that … um … I might want to talk to your parents."

Harper stilled, the hair on the back of her neck standing on end. "My parents? Why?" She tried to keep her voice neutral, but she couldn't stop her stomach from twisting.

"Apparently Tess worked at a bar that your father frequented quite often," Jared replied, sympathy rolling over him. "She was known to get chummy with the guests."

"Did Mel tell you that?" Harper's tone was accusatory.

"Mel said that Tess was rumored to have hooked up with a lot of people at the bar and then he mentioned that your father spent a lot of time at the bar," Jared said, choosing his words carefully. He was really starting to wish he'd never broached the subject with Harper and instead approached her father by himself. "Mel said he didn't know if your father had an affair with her, just that they'd been seen around town together a time or two."

"My father would never cheat on my mother."

"I didn't say he did."

"That's not the way he is," Harper said, her voice firm. "I know my parents are … eccentric … but we don't believe in cheating on significant others in the Harlow family."

"That's good to know," Jared said. "I don't believe in that either. I'm not accusing your father of anything."

"That's not how it sounds to me."

Jared sighed as he pinched the bridge of his nose. She was backing him into a corner and he didn't like it. "Heart, I don't want to upset you. In fact, that's the last thing I want. Forget I brought it up. I'm sorry."

"Oh, it's too late for that," Harper said, annoyed. "What do you want to do? Surely you can't believe that my father killed her to cover up an affair and then buried her on Annette's property and somehow hid the photos in her attic."

Jared's eyes widened. "Wow. That's a wild leap. When did I say that?"

Harper crossed her arms over her chest, her stubbornness coming out to play. "That's what I heard."

"Then clean out your ears," Jared instructed. "I don't for one second believe your father had anything to do with this. As you pointed out yourself, him being responsible wouldn't exactly make a lot of sense."

"Oh." Harper was marginally placated. "What were you getting at then?"

"I was hoping you could set up a dinner with your father," Jared replied, fighting the urge to shake his head. Just when he thought he had a grasp on women and their emotions, Harper managed to throw him into a tailspin. "I thought I could get to know him better and ask him about Tess. If it's in a casual environment he's less likely to feel pressured."

"Oh, well, I don't see why we can't do that," Harper said, brightening considerably. "When do you want me to set it up?"

"How does tonight sound?"

"Doable."

"Great." Jared internally sighed in relief as he leaned back in his chair. "You're a lot of work. You know that, right?"

"I'm totally worth it, though."

Despite his agitation, Jared couldn't help but grin. "You are totally worth it," he agreed. "Pick a good restaurant tonight. I'll prove how much you're worth it by splurging on an expensive meal."

"That's the best offer I've had all day."

"Just wait until you see what I'm offering after dinner."

"Yay!" Harper clapped her hands and moved them away from the table as the waitress delivered their hamburgers. "Finally something to look forward to."

Nine

"Did you see any sign that Zander returned to the house after work?"

Harper's mind was jumbled, too many threads warring for supremacy as she fussed with the small purse on her lap. She didn't know if she should focus on Zander's secret date, dinner with her father, the dead woman, or Jared's awesome butt. She was truly at a loss.

"I have no idea." Jared leaned back in the driver's seat of his truck as he stopped at a light. He adored Harper beyond reason, but her insistence on obsessing about Zander was starting to grate. "How about we focus on us instead of Zander tonight? How does that sound?"

"I ... oh." Harper pursed her lips. She hadn't realized how close to the edge Jared was leaning until it was almost too late. "I'm sorry. I promise I'll be good."

Jared snorted as he captured Harper's hand and pressed a kiss to the palm. She was a ball of nerves, and only some of it had to do with Zander. He couldn't blame her for being anxious. "It's okay," he said after a moment's consideration. "You can pay me back with a massage later."

"Okay. I want a massage, too, though."

"Oh, no." Jared shook his head, laughter lighting his eyes as Harper's lower lip jutted out. "When I keep you up late for a reason other than ... kissing ... I give you a massage. When the roles are reversed, you owe me."

"I kept you up last night? How?" Harper was legitimately surprised. She assumed Jared slept heavy – like he usually did – and missed her constant mumbling.

"You're not nearly as sly as you think you are," Jared replied, squeezing her hand. "You were up and down out of the bed so many times I lost count."

"I was just checking to see if Zander came out. He could've been in an accident or something. I was simply being a dedicated roommate."

Jared made an exaggerated face as he rolled his eyes. "Don't lie to me, woman. You wanted to catch him coming in. I'm not an idiot. You were planning on jumping out of a dark corner and grilling him."

"That is not true."

Jared patiently waited.

"Fine, that's mostly true," Harper conceded. "He always tells me about his dates, though. There has to be something wrong with this guy for him to be hiding it … and I'm talking 'ax murderer' not 'he's got a mole on his lip' wrong. If the mole was the only thing we had to grapple with, he would tell me."

"Oh, geez." Jared shook his head as he pulled into the parking lot at the local seafood restaurant. He let Harper pick where she wanted to have dinner and she answered almost immediately. She was a huge fan of surf and turf and Jared had no problem forking over the funds for a big meal if it would make her happy. Unfortunately for both of them, she was anything but happy. "You know, Heart, only a woman would jump to a bad conclusion without any proof. I thought you were better than that." He was trying to bully her out of her bad mood – or at least force her to put on a good face for spite – but it backfired.

"Zander would jump to that conclusion," Harper countered. "Do you remember when you left town before we even had our official first date?"

"Oh, I should've seen this coming," Jared groused. "I thought you weren't going to bring that up again. That was an honest mistake."

Harper ignored his whining. "While you were out of town Zander suggested that you had another family on the west side of the state," she supplied. "He said we would have to watch you closely for signs of being a bigamist."

"Yes, that sounds totally plausible," Jared drawled, killing the truck's ignition and pushing open his door. "I can barely keep up with you, Heart. Adding another woman to this particular mix would be unrealistic and unbearable."

Harper wasn't sure, but she was fairly convinced that was meant as an insult. "Hey, I'm talking to you," she complained, hopping out of the truck and stopping at the rear of the vehicle to straighten her skirt. "I wasn't even close to being done."

Jared watched her, amused, and merely shook his head. "You're done with the Zander rant," he said, extending his hand. "I don't want our entire night to be about Zander. I know you don't see the problem with it, but I'm not nearly as fascinated with Zander as you seem to be."

Harper made a disgusted sound in the back of her throat as she slipped her hand in his. "You make it sound as if I'm obsessed."

"You're totally obsessed," Jared said, tugging her closer so he could skim her cheek with his finger. "You're also beautiful. You look lovely tonight. You don't wear skirts very often. I forgot how much I like seeing your legs."

Harper wanted to be agitated with the backhanded compliment, but she couldn't help but warm to his touch.

"Thank you. I can't wear skirts to work because I always end up dirty."

"Then I guess I'm going to have to take you out more often."

"I guess so."

Jared planted a smoldering kiss on Harper, sharing a preview of what he had planned for later in the evening. He was happy to sink into the exchange until he heard the distinctive sound of a man clearing his throat. When Jared swiveled, he found Phil Harlow staring at him.

"I see I missed the appetizers," Phil said dryly.

"Hi, Dad." Harper separated from Jared and gave her father an affectionate hug. "How are you?"

"Happy that you remembered you have a father," Phil replied, his eyes hopping to Jared. "How are you?"

Jared recovered quickly. He wasn't keen on Phil seeing him put the moves on his only daughter, but Harper was an adult. Jared refused to be embarrassed for showing affection. "I'm good, sir. How are you?" Jared extended his hand in greeting.

Phil eyed the man's hand for a moment, a small smile playing at the corner of his lips. "That hand hasn't been anywhere bad, has it?"

It took Jared a moment to realize what Phil was referring to. "Of course not!"

"Dad, don't mess with him," Harper warned, her voice low. "He's already nervous enough as it is."

"It's a father's prerogative to mess with his daughter's male suitor," Phil countered. "I didn't get much of a chance while you were in high school because you didn't date a lot and Zander refuses to get embarrassed."

"Yes, well, that is one of his finer qualities," Harper said, linking her arm through her father's and tugging him toward the door. "Thank you for agreeing to meet us on such short notice, by the way. I wasn't sure if you would be busy or not."

"I didn't have anything on my slate besides going through the itemized divorce list. Your mother is trying to steal my murder mystery book collection, by the way. She thought she could slip it through. I showed her, though. I demanded she split apart her romances if she wanted a piece of my mysteries. She backed right off."

Harper pressed her lips together and raised her eyebrows. Her parents' marriage survived more fights than kisses when she was growing up. She always thought they were on the brink of divorce. They surprised her by waiting until she was an adult and then embarking on the most contentious divorce in history. They filed a multitude of months before and were still haggling over silverware and masking tape. Harper had no idea what to make of it. They both seemed to thrive on the drama, though.

"Well, good for you," Harper said, patting his arm before locking gazes with Jared. "Is everyone ready for a great meal?"

"I can't wait," Phil answered. "Your mother would never let me eat steak because red meat is supposedly bad for you, but I'm eating an entire cow tonight."

Jared rubbed the corner of his mouth with his thumb as he fought to maintain an even demeanor. "I think we're all excited."

"SO, YOU two look all … shiny."

Phil waited until everyone had their drinks and orders placed before addressing Jared. He couldn't help but enjoy the man's occasional bout of discomfort.

"Shiny?" Harper, unlike Jared, was used to her father's machinations. She knew when he was playing a game, and he was clearly playful tonight.

"You know what I mean," Phil said. "You're awestruck when you look at one another. It's kind of cute."

"Awestruck?" Jared chuckled as he sipped his wine. "That's an odd word to choose."

"Is it wrong?"

"No. I'm awed every time I look at your daughter."

"Oh, that was a ridiculously good answer," Phil said, grinning when he saw the way Harper's cheeks flushed with color. "My kid seems to like it, too. You guys seem to be getting along well."

"Did you think we weren't?" Harper asked, confused.

"No, I just worried that your job might get in the way," Phil hedged. "I'm glad to see that Jared doesn't let that bother him."

Harper knew her father well enough to know he was really trying to feel out Jared regarding the ghosts. When she was a young child her parents didn't believe in her ability. Eventually they came to accept what she could do, but it wasn't without effort on everyone's part.

"Dad wants to know if you're embarrassed by my job," Harper supplied.

"That's not true," Phil protested, irked. "I just said that I admire him for being able to look past your job. There's a difference."

"Not really, but I'll take your word for it," Harper said dryly, fighting the urge to roll her eyes.

"Her job doesn't bother me," Jared offered. "Sure, there are elements of it that worry me. I don't like the idea of her putting herself in dangerous situations. That makes me sick to my stomach sometimes when I think about it. As for the other stuff, well, your daughter is gifted. She's good at what she does and offers a valuable service. How could that ever embarrass me?"

"And that's another good answer," Phil said, impressed. "I like you."

Jared's lips twitched. "I like you, too."

"Better than Gloria?"

Gloria Harlow was Harper's mother. Jared had only conversed with the woman a few times – and one of those times was genuinely unpleasant – but he couldn't muster overt dislike for the woman.

"I like you both the same," Jared answered.

"Well, I'm liking you less now," Phil muttered, shaking his head. "Let's talk about something else. Tell me what you've been up to, kid."

Harper shrugged. "Janet Markowitz says her sister is haunting her barn."

"Janet Markowitz is a crackhead."

"Dad!" Harper shook her head in mock scolding. "She's old. She clearly doesn't do crack."

"The whole family was a dime short of a dollar if you ask me," Phil said. "They were all insulated and did crazy stuff out there. There was a rumor that the parents were really brother and sister."

Harper's stomach flipped. "Is that true?"

"I don't think so, but a lot of those kids were slow."

"Janet told me her brother got crushed while cow tipping and became a cow pancake," Harper said. "I can see how people would think they're slow."

Phil barked out a laugh, amused. "I heard you were out at Annette Fleming's place the other day, too. Someone says you found a body."

Harper couldn't help but tense when he brought up the subject. Was he fishing for information? Was he genuinely curious. "I ... ."

"Annette Fleming found photos of a dead body in her attic," Jared interjected smoothly, resting his hand on top of Harper's on the tabletop. "She wanted us to take a look. We didn't find anything in the attic, but Harper saw a ... friend ... from the upstairs window and we followed her into the woods."

"A friend?" Phil leaned forward, intrigued. "Oh, a *friend*. Do you know who it is?"

Jared answered almost immediately. "Tess Hilliard."

"Tess?" Phil screwed up his face into an unreadable expression. "Are you kidding? The rumor was she took off with some guy who approached her at the bar. Everyone believed it because she had a certain ... reputation."

Harper let loose with a shaky breath. Despite her bravado earlier, she was relieved that her father seemed genuinely puzzled over the turn of events.

"We're sure," Jared confirmed. "She's dead and we're almost positive she's the woman in the photos."

"Who took the photos?"

"We have no idea," Jared replied. "The easy answer is Arthur, but he's dead so we can't question him."

"But how did Arthur hook up with Tess?"

"According to the files, Tess was very popular," Jared explained. "Maybe they had an affair that no one knew about."

"It's true that Tess would sleep with anyone who had a pulse, but she wasn't a bad woman," Phil said. "She once helped me do a gardening project as a surprise Mother's Day gift for Gloria. She was a hard worker. She never hit on me once."

Jared and Harper exchanged a quick look. That would explain why people saw Phil and Tess together over such a limited time period.

"Did she ever confide in you?" Jared asked. "Did she ever say if she was having trouble with a man … or heck, a man's wife, for that matter?"

"She was never one to complain about her troubles," Phil said. "She was a nice woman who had issues. I'm sorry to hear that she's dead, though. I always hoped she found some sort of happiness when she left town. Now it turns out she never left town."

"And you're sure Arthur had no ties to her?" Harper pressed.

"Arthur didn't have ties to anyone but himself," Phil replied. "He was a downright disagreeable man. You've met Annette. I'm sure you can see why."

"And here I thought he made Annette disagreeable," Jared mused.

"I guess it's possible they made each other disagreeable," Phil said. "They were extremely unhappy, though. I never knew them to be happy. I also never knew Arthur to step out on Annette. It wasn't as if they were devoted to each other, but it wasn't as if he was getting affection anywhere else either."

"Can you think of anyone Tess spent a lot of time with back in the day?" Harper asked.

"I can't, but I'll give it some thought," Phil said. If he suspected the couple invited him to dinner so they could grill him about his relationship with Tess, he didn't let on. "I would check out that bar just over the Algonac line. That's where Tess worked and a lot of regulars still go there."

"I'll definitely do that," Jared said, relaxing into his chair. "Thank you for the tip."

"Don't mention it," Phil said, turning his attention to Harper. "So, tell me what's going on with you and Zander. I hear tell you're fighting."

Harper's mouth dropped open. "Who told you that?"

"This town is thick with gossip, kid. Everyone is talking about it."

"Nothing is going on," Harper replied. "We're fine."

"How come I don't believe you?"

"Because you're an untrustworthy soul," Harper shot back. "How are things with you and Mom?"

"That woman is the devil. I don't want to talk about her."

"You always want to talk about her."

Phil scowled before allowing his gaze to land on Jared. "Women are evil, son. I know she's my daughter and I genuinely love her, but you need to be careful with this one. She'll sucker you in with that smile and then – bam! – the next thing you know she'll be trying to steal your Lee Child novels."

Jared pursed his lips, amused. "I'll keep that in mind. Something tells me I'm going to be okay on that front, though. I don't even like reading mysteries."

Harper elbowed him in the stomach. "Don't encourage him."

"I was being serious. I would give up all of my murder mysteries for you."

Harper's smile was small but heartfelt. "That was another good answer. You're on a roll tonight."

"Just wait until later. I'm going to totally wow you."

"I can't wait."

TEN

"Janet Markowitz called and wants to know when we're going to be out to deal with her ghost issue."

Harper wasn't fond of mornings – she fully believed her brain didn't start firing on all cylinders until after noon most days – but Eric's greeting the next day was enough to set her teeth on edge.

The man sat at the small table in the corner of the room working on a piece of equipment – Harper was too tired to figure out what it was – and Harper scorched glare holes in the back of his head as she rested her gourmet coffee cup on her desk. Whisper Cove was too small for a Starbucks but the local coffee shop was just as good.

"We have to modify the dreamcatcher," Harper said wearily. "I'll do that this afternoon. A poltergeist is more difficult than a ghost. We told her that yesterday."

"Yes, well, she seems to think we're lazing about on our fat rear ends," Eric intoned. "Those are her words, mind you. She actually used them when talking to me."

"She's a piece of work," Harper grumbled.

"She's ten pieces of work … and all of them wear overalls."

Despite her fatigue, Harper couldn't help but smile. Dinner with her father and Jared lasted for hours, her father finally giving in to his inner urges and spending two hours going on what felt like the world's longest diatribe about Gloria Harlow. He wrapped up his rant that included a conspiracy theory that somehow centered around Gloria being a Russian spy, and she was so disliked by the mother country they didn't want her back so she was forced to remain in the United States or risk death by firing squad. Harper couldn't really remember most of the highlights, but Jared was laughing so hard when they got back to the house she indulged him in a fiery game of "Where are the confidential documents hidden?" before passing out from sheer exhaustion.

Harper was in a good mood when she woke. She was warm and comfortable, Jared's body wrapped around hers, and it was only after five minutes of quiet contemplation that she remembered the Zander issue. She was determined to talk to him over breakfast about his hidden date (and any other illicit activities he may have failed to mention to her), but that never manifested because he'd already left for work when she rose. He was obviously avoiding her. There could be no other explanation.

"I'll make sure to get the dreamcatcher done today," Harper said. "We need to come up with a plan, though. Poltergeists are much stronger than ghosts and there's a lot of dangerous stuff in that barn that a poltergeist could toss our way during a fight. I think it would be safer to draw the ghost out rather than fight on her terms."

"I'm game for whatever you come up with," Eric said. "Just give me a heads-up so we can approach it with a solid plan. A diagram of what you're thinking couldn't hurt either."

"I'll make sure Zander puts something together." Harper scanned the office, tilting her head to the side as she furrowed her brow. "Speaking of Zander, where is he? Did he run out for doughnuts without me?"

Eric stilled, his eyes flashing surprise as they locked with hers. "He called in sick."

"I'm sorry … what?" Harper was convinced Eric made a mistake.

"He called in sick," Eric repeated. "The message was on the company voicemail. I checked the messages for new clients when I came in and he was the only one on there. He said he had the flu or something but would work on the billing and financial files from home."

Harper didn't know how to respond. Her heart rate sped up at she pressed her lips together and stared at the back wall of the office. "He called in sick?"

"Are you telling me you didn't know?" Eric was understandably confused. "You guys live together."

"He wasn't home when I left this morning," Harper replied, her stomach twisting. "In fact, I'm not sure if he came home at all last night. I just assumed he was in bed when Jared and I got back from eating dinner with my father."

"Oh, well, I wouldn't worry about it." Eric said the words, but his eyes reflected doubt. "He probably met a guy at the gym. We'll spend the next three days hearing about hairy bellybuttons and suspect hairlines."

"Uh-huh." Harper fought overtime to maintain a façade of professionalism. She only managed the feat for thirty seconds before her emotions went into overdrive. "He's up to something."

"I ... don't know what to say," Eric admitted, his cheeks crimson. He wasn't used to Harper and Zander being anything other than in sync. Even when they had their occasional fights they were still close. This was something entirely different. "Do you want me to call him?"

"Oh, no," Harper intoned, shaking her head as an evil expression took hold of her face. "I'll take care of Zander. You keep working on ... whatever it is you're working on." Harper turned on her heel and stalked toward the door. "I'll be on my cell phone if you need me. You're in charge of the office today."

Eric remained dubious. "Can you call Molly and tell her that? She never listens to me."

Harper ignored the question. She was already focused on Zander and his newfound ability to lie to her. "Sick? I'll show you sick, buddy. You're going to wish you never met me."

"OH, GEEZ."

Jared leaned his head back and rubbed the tender spot between his eyebrows as he stared at the ceiling over his desk. He held his cell phone in one hand – a fresh text from Harper scrolling across the screen – and gripped the arm of his desk chair with the other.

"What's wrong?" Mel asked, his eyes flashing as he strolled into the room. "You look as if you'd rather be anywhere else but here."

"That's a standard feeling, in case you're interested, but I would definitely prefer being here than anywhere else today," Jared replied.

"Meaning?"

"Meaning that I'm sick and tired of Harper and Zander's crap. Do you know what kind of text she just sent me?" Jared was normally fairly unflappable, but he couldn't seem to get a handle on his roiling emotions. He held out the phone and waved it in Mel's face. "Do you have any clue what she just sent me?"

"If it's filthy then I don't want to see it," Mel answered, shoving the phone away.

"It's not a dirty text," Jared barked.

Mel reluctantly took the phone and snickered as he read the message out loud. "Zander called in sick and yet he's not at home. I'm going to figure out where he is and make him wish he was sick."

"Isn't that crazy?" Jared was beyond agitated. "I'm in a relationship with a crazy person. I'm crazy about a crazy person. This is all on me really. I saw the signs and did nothing about them."

"She's not crazy," Mel countered. "Er, well, she's not completely crazy. What's the deal with her and Zander? They usually don't fight for more than twenty-four hours. Is he really sick? He's a total baby when he's sick and generally wants Harper to wait on him."

"He's not sick," Jared replied. "He's dating someone and not telling Harper about it. I think her brain is going to combust or something."

Mel's face was blank as he stared at Jared. "There's no way he's dating someone and not talking to Harper about it. That's what they do."

"Yes, well, there's something different about this situation," Jared said. "We saw them at the grocery store the other day and Harper has been trying to trick Zander into admitting what he's doing – and with whom – but he's being unusually tight-lipped."

"Oh, well, that's not like him at all," Mel said, scratching his cheek as he mulled over the problem. "I wonder why he's keeping this from Harper. There must be something wrong with the guy, like 'I chopped up my ex-boyfriend and buried him in the backyard' wrong and not 'I haven't trimmed my nose hairs in seven years' wrong."

Jared's mouth dropped open. "You sound like Harper sometimes."

Mel preened. "I'll take that as a compliment."

"I'm pretty sure she's crazy right now," Jared reminded him.

"Well, son, you can't win them all," Mel said, clapping Jared on the back. "If I were you I would stay out of this situation. Things are obviously going to come to a head between those two – and soon. When it happens, you don't want to be in the impact zone. It's going to get ugly."

That was exactly what Jared was afraid of.

"HEY, HARPER."

Meredith Stevens stood behind the library counter and flashed a bright smile when Harper edged into the building shortly after noon. The welcoming expression only lasted for a few seconds, and when Harper didn't answer – and instead plastered her face against the side window so she could stare at the building next door – Meredith quietly closed the distance between the two women. She leaned over, placing her hands on her knees, and stared across the side street.

"What are we looking at?"

Harper jumped. She had no idea Meredith was so close. "I … nothing." Harper straightened and rolled her neck. "I wasn't looking at anything."

"You were staring out the window and looking at nothing?" Meredith didn't look convinced. She'd gone to high school with Zander and Harper – graduated one year behind them, in fact – and she was well aware that the gregarious blonde had a few odd quirks. "Why don't I believe you?"

"I have no idea," Harper replied, blithe. "I have a very trustworthy face."

Meredith giggled, genuinely amused. "So how are things? I see you around town with that hot cop all of the time. You two seem happy."

Harper mustered a real smile at mention of Jared. "I'm very happy. He's … great."

"He looks great," Meredith said. "I wish I would've seen him first."

"Yes, well, I would've still had to fight you for him," Harper teased, leaning against one of the display shelves. "What are you doing here today? I thought Donna would be here and I would have to make up a story about what I was doing so she wouldn't tell my mother I was acting squirrelly. That's her word, by the way, not mine."

Meredith giggled, amused. "Donna is at a doctor's appointment today so I volunteered to run the library for the afternoon. It's an easy gig and I can relax without anyone bothering me."

"Nothing is wrong with Donna, right?" Harper couldn't help but be worried. "She's mean, but I still like her."

"It's just a checkup," Meredith said, waving off Harper's concern. "That woman is built like a tank. She'll outlive all of us."

"That's true." Harper sucked in a breath as she glanced around. "So … you're probably wondering what I'm doing."

"Not really," Meredith replied dryly. "Zander's car is at the gym across the street and I figured you two were doing … something … the rest of us would never understand. That's your way."

"Oh, well, it's nice that you understand me," Harper said, patting Meredith's arm. "He just went inside a few minutes ago, though, and he's going to be there at least an hour. While I'm here, I need to look at some old newspapers."

"Sure," Meredith said, bobbing her head. "What are you looking for?"

"Anything you have on the disappearance of Tess Hilliard," Harper replied, trailing Meredith to the microfiche room. "She disappeared twenty-five years ago and her body just turned up."

"Oh, is that the body you and the hot cop discovered by the Fleming house?" Meredith asked, intrigued. "That was the talk of the diner this morning. Everyone thinks it's weird that you guys just magically discovered it."

Harper did her best to ignore the suspicious tilt of Meredith's head. "I don't know if I would call it magic. Annette asked us to go to the house because she found photographs that looked as if they were of a dead body. We were searching the attic, but there's no freaking air conditioning in that house, so Jared and I decided to walk by the river. Her hand was sticking out of the ground right by the banks."

Meredith made a horrified face. "Oh, man. That's terrible."

"I didn't even realize what we were looking at until Jared told me," Harper lied. Meredith was a nice woman but a terrible gossip. Harper wanted to put her in control of the rumor mill so suspicions would ease. "We were just sitting in the shade and he was like ... 'oh, crap.'"

"I guess that ruined a romantic break, huh?" Meredith shook her head and made a clucking sound in the back of her throat. "Did you have nightmares?"

"Not really. It wasn't like a body. It was just bones. It was still creepy."

"I'll bet." Meredith sat at the microfiche machine. "Okay, so we're looking at stuff from twenty-five years ago and anything that has to do with Tess Hilliard, right?"

Harper nodded as she watched the woman work. "While you're at it, see if you can dig up anything on Arthur Fleming."

Meredith's eyes widened. "Do you think he's responsible?"

"I think photos of a dead woman were in that attic and then a body showed up on the property," Harper replied. "That can't be a coincidence."

"Definitely not. Let's see what we can find."

"WELL, IT seems as if Tess Hilliard was barely a blip as far as the local news media was concerned," Meredith said forty-five minutes later. "That's kind of a bummer, huh?"

"It's definitely a bummer," Harper said, resting her chin on her hand as she stared at the screen. "They did like two stories about her ... and both were only a few paragraphs. I know it was a different time, but that's still depressing."

"Yeah, if I go missing, I hope someone looks for me longer than five minutes."

"I'll look for you," Harper said, patting her hand. "What about Arthur? Did you find anything on him?"

"Most of the stuff on Arthur is nuisance complaints," Meredith replied, shifting screens. "In 1993 alone he appeared in the police blotter eight times."

"Really?" Harper's eyebrows flew up her forehead. "For what?"

"Not for murder, if that's what you're worried about," Meredith answered, chuckling. "Most of it was weird stuff … like pulling a gun on trespassers, threatening local hunters who were baiting deer on his property, running over his neighbor's mailbox. You know … petty stuff."

"As far as I can tell no one liked the guy," Harper mused. "I guess I shouldn't be surprised by the other stuff."

"No, I can't ever remember him even being mildly nice," Meredith said. "We used to dare each other to knock on the Flemings' door for Halloween when I was a kid because we were scared of him."

"We all did that."

"Yeah, well, I got up the courage to do it one time and when he opened the door he stole my candy."

Harper didn't want to laugh – she was sure it was a traumatic ordeal for a child – but she couldn't help herself. "He was a cantankerous old coot."

"He was evil," Meredith said. "Although … there is one interesting thing. Look here."

Harper followed Meredith's finger with her eyes. "Local man saves woman and child from fire," she read the headline aloud. "That was Arthur?"

"Yeah. Apparently he ran into a burning building and carried out the woman and child. He saved them both."

"That doesn't sound anything like him."

"I think it proves that there is good in everyone," Meredith said, smiling. "I don't know what else to tell you. That's all we have on Arthur or Tess."

"Which isn't much," Harper muttered, rubbing her chin. "I don't know what to make of any of this. It's just so … odd."

"Well, good luck," Meredith said. "If anyone can solve it, I'm sure it's you. Just don't neglect the hot cop while you're at it. It would be a shame to lose that face."

"His butt is even better," Harper teased, getting to her feet. "Thank you for your time."

"Don't mention it. Let me know if you decide to cut the cop loose. I want to be ready to move in quick if it happens."

Harper merely shook her head. "I don't ever want to cut him loose."

Meredith heaved out a sigh. "I figured. It was worth a shot, though. I guess I'm stuck with my dreams. You're a lucky woman."

"I tell myself that every single day." Harper's face took on a dreamy expression until she caught a hint of movement outside the window. "Ha! Zander is moving. I'm totally going to crush him."

Meredith watched with bemused eyes as Harper raced toward the door. "She may be weird, but I'm still jealous," the woman muttered to herself. "So very, very jealous."

ELEVEN

"What's up, honey bear?"

Jared pocketed his keys as he hopped out of his truck later that night, grinning as he crossed Harper's lawn. She stood in front of the porch, hands on hips, and frowned. The expression caused him to pull up short.

"Oh, geez," he muttered, rubbing his hand over his short-cropped hair. "What's going on now?"

"What makes you think anything is going on?" Harper asked, defensive.

"I can tell by the look on your face," Jared replied. "I haven't heard from you all afternoon. The last text you sent was right after lunch. You said you were going to the library to do research."

"That's what I did."

Jared wanted to believe her, but he was understandably dubious. "What did you really do?"

"Research."

"And?"

"It just so happens that the library is located next to the gym," Harper explained, averting her gaze. "Zander magically showed up. I guess he wasn't too sick for a trip to the gym."

"Ah." Jared pressed the heel of his hand to his forehead. "I'm guessing that he wasn't alone."

"No, his grocery store gigolo was with him."

"Grocery store gigolo?" Jared was beyond weary of Harper's ridiculous attitude regarding Zander's dating habits, but he couldn't help but crack a smile. "I see your head is in a really good place right now. I think that's going to mean great things for our night together. What do you want to do for dinner?"

Harper's face twisted into an expression Jared had never seen before. "Dinner? We're not worrying about dinner right now."

"But I'm hungry."

"You need to move your truck," Harper instructed. "Put it behind the storage building. Hopefully Zander won't see it right away."

"Why?"

"Because I want Zander to think the house is empty."

"Why?"

Harper heaved out a long-suffering sigh. She had no idea how Jared could be such an effective cop when he couldn't even keep up with a simple conversation. "I texted Zander and told him I was spending the night at your house. He's going to know I'm lying if he sees your vehicle. That's why I parked my car behind the shed. I don't want him to know we're here."

"Uh-huh." Jared licked his lips. "Do you think a trip to a mental health professional would be beneficial for whatever it is you're dealing with right now? I'm willing to pay and offer absolutely no judgment."

On any other day Harper might've been upset or even hurt by Jared's words. Now she could barely focus on them, though. "Put your truck behind the shed."

"Given your mood, perhaps I should just go home." Jared hadn't meant for the words to resemble a threat, but that's exactly how they came out.

Harper crossed her arms over her chest, her lower lip stubbornly jutting out. "Fine. If that's what you want, well, I guess I can't stop you. I thought you wanted to help me, but I guess that's not the case."

Instead of melting and professing his undying loyalty, Jared merely scowled. "Oh, that's cute. You're trying to manipulate me."

"I'm not trying to manipulate you," Harper clarified. "I'm trying to boss you around. There's a difference."

It wasn't an amusing situation – er, well, mostly – but Jared couldn't stop the smile from spreading across his face. "What's your plan, ace?"

"You're going to hide your truck behind the shed and then we're going to sit behind those bushes over there," Harper replied, pointing to the shaped shrubs on the east side of the house. "Zander is going to bring his grocery store gigolo here and when he does I'm going to jump out of the bushes and pull his hair until he tells me what's going on."

"I see." Jared linked his fingers in front of him as he considered the plan. "What if Zander doesn't bring his boyfriend here?"

"He will."

"How do you know that?"

"I also might've texted him that his favorite shirt was in the bathroom and I left it there while I showered."

"I have no idea why that's important."

"The shirt is dry clean only and the ventilation in that bathroom is nonexistent."

"Oh, well, that makes perfect sense," Jared intoned, shaking his head. "If I do this with you, do you promise to make sure I get fed? I'm not sitting in those bushes for more than an hour either way, though."

"He'll be here in less than thirty minutes."

"And how do you know that?"

"Trust me."

Jared made a popping sound as he worked his lips together and then finally shook his head as he turned back to his truck. "I have no idea why I'm doing this. It's clear you're crazy. I think you've made me crazy. There's no other explanation. Apparently crazy is catchy." He muttered the words to himself, but Harper clearly heard them.

"Thank you," she called to his back.

"You're massaging the crap out of me tonight."

"Consider it done."

STOP DOING that."

"I'm not doing anything."

"You're kissing my ear."

"You're imagining things."

"I know what a tongue in my ear feels like." Harper drew her eyes together and offered Jared her sternest face as he shifted to get more comfortable on the ground. "No funny business. Zander will be here any second."

"You've been saying that for twenty minutes," Jared pointed out. "I wasn't joking when I said you have an hour. If Zander isn't here in forty minutes you're going to have to cook dinner for me … and I would prefer it if you were naked while doing it."

Harper made an exaggerated face that was just adorable enough to earn another kiss. "I'm thinking steak and corn," Jared said. "Maybe some mushrooms and onions. We both have to eat the onions, though. That way no one will complain about stinky breath."

"Zander is coming," Harper said, although she didn't pull away when Jared nuzzled her neck. "He'll be here any second." She rubbed her hand over Jared's muscular shoulders and sighed. "This is nice. Didn't I tell you this would be nice?"

"This is only nice because I'm keeping it interesting," Jared replied, his teeth grazing her jaw line. "It's a warm night, too. Thankfully it's not too humid. I don't want to deal with sweat until later."

"You're a sick man sometimes."

"I have my moments. I … ." Jared didn't get a chance to finish his sentence because a pair of headlights bounced off their hiding space as a car pulled into the driveway. Jared rolled to his stomach, curious despite himself, and watched as Zander hopped out of the driver's seat. He wasn't alone. The handsome man from the grocery store was with him.

"I told you," Harper hissed, her voice low as her predatory gaze latched onto Zander.

"This will just take a second," Zander offered his friend. "I need to make sure that my shirt is safely locked in my closet."

"Why did you leave it in the bathroom?" the other man asked.

"I didn't. I think Harper is trying to punish me."

Harper frowned as Jared gripped her hand as a form of solidarity.

"Why is she trying to punish you?" the man asked. "I thought you two were best friends."

"We are best friends," Zander confirmed, his keys jangling as he moved toward the porch steps. "She thinks I'm hiding something from her and she always reacts irrationally when that happens."

"You are hiding something from her," the man pointed out. "You're hiding me. I don't understand why you haven't told her about us yet."

"It's just ... not time," Zander said, shaking his head. "I'll know when it's time."

"I hope so," the newcomer said. "I'm looking forward to meeting her."

Jared opened his mouth to whisper a suggestion to Harper, one that wouldn't make her happy given the fact that he wanted to refrain from ambushing Zander. He didn't get a chance, though, because Harper was already on her feet.

Zander was taken aback when he saw her pop up on the side of the porch. "Harp?"

"I've got you now, you big, fat liar!"

"Don't you dare call me fat!" Zander shot back.

Jared rolled his neck as he struggled to a sitting position and met the newcomer's wary gaze. "So, who wants steak with our heaping pile of finger pointing and tears?"

I'M SHAWN Donavan." Zander's friend looked uncertain as he glanced between angry faces. "I've heard a lot of wonderful things about you."

"Now probably isn't the time," Jared said, resting his hand on Shawn's shoulder and directing him to the far side of the kitchen island. "Things are about to get loud. You don't want to get in the middle of it."

"Should I leave?" Shawn looked uncertain. "My place is only a few blocks away and I can walk."

"That will just make things worse," Jared replied. "You can help me with dinner preparations. Do you like steak and corn?"

Shawn nodded.

"Then we'll get along fine. I'm Jared Monroe, by the way."

"You're Harper's boyfriend," Shawn said, licking his lips. He kept one eye on Harper and Zander as they glared at each other but seemed almost relieved to stick close to Jared and have a conversation – no matter how mundane – to focus on. "Zander has told me a lot about you."

"If he's mentioned my nipples, I'm going to beat the crap out of him."

Despite the tense situation, Shawn burst out laughing. "I think I'm going to like you."

"I'm pretty sure I'm going to like you, too," Jared said. "No matter what's about to happen, though, keep an open mind. This has been building for days. You're not really meeting Harper at her best. She needs to embrace the derangement before she can clear her head and be civil."

"Okay."

Zander's cheeks burned as he fisted his hands and locked gazes with his lifelong best friend. "How could you?"

"How could I what?" Harper matched him dark look for dark look.

"Lie to me," Zander replied. "You made me think my favorite shirt was in imminent peril."

"That's on you," Harper replied airily. "If you'd been here over the past twenty-four hours you would've known that your shirt was safely locked in your closet, right between your paisley button-down and alpaca sweater like it always is."

"You lied to me," Zander snapped. "You said you were spending the night at Jared's house and that my shirt was in danger. That's two lies, in fact. So … liar, liar, pants on fire."

Harper narrowed her eyes to dangerous blue slits. She seemed oblivious to the other men in the room, but Jared knew that was far from true because she keenly felt Shawn's presence. She wanted to study him up close. She had to deal with Zander first.

"Do you really want to talk about lying?" Harper challenged, the corners of her mouth curling into a demented sneer. "You, the man who was at the grocery store with your … new friend … the other night, do you want to talk about lying?"

Zander balked. "I never lied. How do you even know we were there?"

"Because we saw you while we were shopping," Jared replied. "I really wouldn't pick that hill to die on, dude. We saw you and there's no getting out of that. She's been worked up ever since."

"Marinate the steaks, Jared!" Harper barked.

Jared and Shawn exchanged amused glances before focusing on their task.

"If you really wanted to know, you should've asked me," Zander said. "I would've told you everything. Not volunteering information isn't the same thing as lying."

Harper was beside herself. "You called in sick today."

"I had the flu."

"You didn't come home last night."

"I was … otherwise engaged."

Harper tugged on her ear to calm herself. She was very close to blowing a gasket. "You were at the gym this afternoon. How are you working out when you're so close to death's door?"

Zander's mouth dropped open. "You were spying on me?"

"I was at the library doing research," Harper countered. That was kind of true. She only decided to do the research after discovering his car. He didn't need to know that, though. "I looked through the window and saw you … with him."

"He has a name," Zander hissed. "It's Shawn."

"I'm referring to him as the 'grocery store gigolo' until you explain why you've been keeping him a secret," Harper snapped. "You always tell me about your dates. If you're hiding this one, there must be something wrong with him. Quick, Jared, search him for drugs."

"I think I'll pass on that," Jared said dryly, gesturing toward a package of mushrooms on the counter. "Shawn, can you chop up an onion? We'll sauté it with the mushrooms."

"Sure."

Harper scorched Jared with a dark look, which he proceeded to ignore.

"I can't believe you, Harp," Zander said, his voice taking on a whiny quality. "We're supposed to be best friends."

"No, best friends confide in one another," Harper countered. "You stopped confiding in me days ago apparently."

"I wonder why."

"Me, too."

"That was a sarcastic rhetorical comment," Zander said. "It was passive aggressive. You should recognize the effort because that's how you roll. You're always passive aggressive, just like when you hemmed and hawed over Jared not wanting me to share your bed."

"Um, I'm a little uncomfortable with the direction this conversation is taking," Shawn said, glancing at Jared for support. "I think I might've misunderstood a few things."

"It's not like that," Jared explained. "Harper and I sleep together and then Zander comes in to gossip in the morning. I have issues with it because of the nudity involved. Harper honestly doesn't mind … and there's no hanky panky."

"Oh, well, that makes me feel a little better," Shawn conceded. "Just for the record, though, are you uncomfortable with her nudity or your own?"

"I think it's a group nudity thing."

"That seems completely fair," Shawn said. "Zander should respect your wishes."

"Thank you." Jared looked vindicated. "I knew I was going to like you, and that was on top of the fact that I realized Zander would be far more likely to stay in his own bed if you hang around this place more often."

"I like you, too," Shawn said, smiling.

"Oh, well, how cute," Zander intoned, making a face. "Your boyfriend is picking up my boyfriend. The night just got worse. I didn't think it was possible."

"Your boyfriend?" Harper was incensed. "You're calling him your boyfriend? I can't even look at you! You refuse to tell me about the guy you're dating and now you're referring to him as your boyfriend? Am I on a television show and no one bothered to tell me?"

"The reason I didn't tell you is because you have a tendency to take over things," Zander shot back. "I didn't want to risk you taking this over."

"I think you have me confused with you."

"Oh, no. You're the bossy one."

"You're the bossy one!"

"You are!"

Jared firmly placed his tongue in his cheek and tilted his head to the side as he picked up the wrapped steaks. "Would you like to help me by the grill, Shawn?"

"You have no idea." Shawn's eyes were still wide when he planted himself next to Jared on the back patio. His gaze flicked in the direction of the house a few times when Zander and Harper's screeches hit a level that would disturb dogs, but Jared made a point of remaining calm.

"Is this going to be okay?" Shawn asked after a beat. "I mean … is their friendship going to survive?"

"Their friendship will survive anything," Jared replied. "It's like a cockroach."

"Tell me how you really feel."

"Okay." Jared rolled his neck as he considered his words. "I really feel that Harper and Zander love each other. I have no idea why Zander didn't tell her about you. You seem like a nice guy. Harper's feelings are hurt because Zander shut her out."

"I figured that out myself," Shawn said. "I don't want to get in the way of their friendship."

"It's going to be okay," Jared said, and to his surprise, he realized that he meant it. "They need to scream at each other and then pout for a bit. Things will work out. You'll see."

"You don't seem worried about this at all."

"I've been around long enough to know that Harper and Zander thrive on the drama," Jared explained. "When the drama wanes, though, they survive on love. It's going to be okay. I promise."

As if on cue, the sound of a glass breaking emanated from the kitchen.

"Just to be on the safe side, though, we're going to eat on paper plates outside," Jared added.

"That sounds like a plan to me."

TWELVE

"And how is everyone this beautiful morning?" Jared dropped a kiss on Harper's cheek before slipping behind the kitchen counter island to pour himself a mug of coffee the next morning. Dinner the previous evening was a pouty affair, and one look at Zander and Harper's faces told Jared that breakfast wasn't going to be much better. "How are you this morning, Shawn? Did you sleep well?"

For his part, the newcomer seemed baffled more than anything else. He sat next to Zander, wearing a T-shirt and boxer shorts, and continuously shifted his gaze between Harper and Zander. "I'm good. These two haven't blinked in more than two minutes, though. I'm starting to think they're possessed."

"Don't worry about it," Jared said, smirking. "Their eyes will dry out eventually. The only thing they're possessed by is stubbornness."

"Uh-huh."

"There're eggs and hash browns on the stove," Zander called out. "I made enough for you, but not for Harper since she's a big, fat stalker."

"Don't call me fat!" Harper snapped.

Jared moseyed over to the stove and lifted the lids off the skillets. There was more than enough for two people. He didn't bother asking before doling out the food onto separate plates and sliding one in front of Harper as he settled at the table.

"This smells great," Jared said, beaming.

"I said that wasn't for her," Zander hissed.

"She needs food because I have a big day planned for her," Jared said. "Do you really want your best friend to starve?"

"She's not my best friend right now. She's the enemy."

"You guys should put a camera in the living room and film your fights for a reality television show," Jared suggested, reaching for the butter. "You'd be rich if you did that. Children everywhere would clap and proclaim you the hip new thing. You'd be like *Gossip Girl*."

Zander and Harper rolled their eyes in unison as Shawn chuckled.

"Do you have a big day today?" Shawn asked, focusing on Jared. He figured that was his safest bet given the mood hovering over the kitchen.

"Yeah, I'm going to interview a woman who Arthur Fleming saved from a fire years ago," Jared answered. "I'm not sure she'll be able to give us anything, but without a cause of death we're still operating in the dark."

"Arthur Fleming saved a woman from a fire?" Zander finally shifted his eyes from Harper. "That doesn't sound like him. He would be far more likely to set the fire."

"And then pull out marshmallows and make s'mores as he watched the house burn to the ground," Harper added.

"I know, right?" For a second Harper and Zander smiled at one another ... and then they remembered their anger. Jared looked at it as a start toward making up.

"Well, I still want to talk to her," Jared said. "There's very little information about Arthur to be gleaned and most of the people he was friends with back in the day have passed away. Mel has been in town his entire life and he says all he can remember about Arthur is that he stole charity money from a jar near the register at the hardware store and he occasionally chased kids off his lawn with a rake."

"Meredith and I went through some old newspaper clippings at the library yesterday," Harper offered. "He was in the police blotter section multiple times for chasing people off his lawn. He used a gun when he did it."

"Maybe that's because he had a body in the woods behind his house and he didn't want anyone to discover it," Zander suggested.

Jared rubbed his thumb over the side of his coffee mug. "That would actually make sense," he said. "Was he always militant about his property, or did it only start after Tess disappeared?"

Harper shrugged. "You said it yourself. We were children when Tess disappeared. We only knew Arthur to be a certain way."

"Mean," Zander said.

"You know it."

Another smile passed between the two and then brows furrowed and they quickly looked away from one another. This time Shawn noticed the interaction and glanced at Jared before hiding his grin.

"I'm not familiar with the players obviously since I just moved to town, but doesn't the widow know anything about this?" Shawn asked. He wanted to keep the conversation rolling.

"Annette is as unpleasant as Arthur was," Zander replied. "If she knows, she's probably willing to take it to her grave."

"That doesn't explain why she brought the photos into the department," Jared pointed out. "If she wanted to keep it a secret, why set off a search in the first place?"

"Maybe she knows she's getting close to the end of her life. Maybe she wanted to scrub the guilt from her soul before she dies."

"Or maybe she had no idea and is really trying to do the right thing," Jared countered.

"We really don't know why she did it. All we know right now is that we have a woman who died twenty-five years ago and a sick individual who took photos of her body before burying it."

"So what's your next step?" Shawn asked. He seemed fascinated by police procedure.

"We talk to the woman who Arthur saved from the fire and then we visit Annette," Jared replied. "I don't know what else to do. If that doesn't work, Phil gave us an idea about checking out a bar that Tess used to work at. We won't be able to do that until tonight, though."

Zander made a face. "When did you see your father?"

"We went out to dinner with him last night," Harper replied.

"Where?"

Harper was smart enough not to answer the question, instead turning her attention to the window over the sink. Jared, on the other hand, didn't recognize the danger until it was too late.

"We went to that seafood place Harper loves," Jared answered. "We stuffed our faces with surf and turf and then listened to Phil explain why Gloria is clearly a Russian spy who was abandoned by the motherland."

Zander's mouth dropped open as Harper fixed Jared with a dirty look.

"What?" Jared asked, confused.

"You promised you would go to that restaurant with me," Zander barked. "That's our favorite place and we haven't been there in forever because you always go with Jared the Jolly Green Friend Stealer."

"Hey!" Jared extended a warning finger. "Do you really want to make an enemy out of me right now, too?"

"Oh, whatever." Zander crossed his arms over his chest. "I'm being betrayed at every turn."

Instead of commiserating with him, Shawn patted Zander's shoulder and made soothing cooing noises. "At least your life isn't dull."

"There is that."

"WHAT'S THIS woman's name?" Harper followed Jared up the pathway to a nondescript two-story Cape Cod home, her eyes roaming the well-kept façade as she matched his speed. She'd been strangely silent during the ride from the neighboring town and Jared didn't want to ruin things by pointing out that she was acting like a baby where Zander was concerned so he wisely kept his mouth shut.

"Helen Slater," Jared replied, pressing his hand to the small of Harper's back as they climbed the steps to the front porch. "I'm going to do most of the talking, but if you think of something important, don't hesitate to ask."

"So … what? Are you giving me permission to talk?"

Jared's smile turned upside down as he knocked on the door. "I'm going to lock you and Zander in a room until you make up if you're not careful. I can't take much more of this attitude."

Harper ignored the grumbling and pasted a bright smile on her face when the door opened. Helen Slater looked to be about fifty and wary. She peered through the latched screen, her suspicious gaze bouncing between Harper and Jared.

"I don't want any cookies."

Harper bit the inside of her cheek to keep from laughing. "Do we look like Girl Scouts?"

Helen shrugged. "I've already found Jesus, too."

"We're actually here to talk to you on an official matter," Jared explained, flashing his badge. "We're investigating an incident involving Arthur Fleming. His name came up in an old file … something about a fire."

"Oh, that?" Helen relaxed when she realized no one was trying to sell her anything and opened the screen door. "That was a long time ago. How is Arthur? I haven't seen him in years, not since I moved from Whisper Cove to New Baltimore, in fact."

"He's dead," Jared replied. "He died a few months ago."

"Oh, that's too bad." Helen looked sad but not altogether surprised at the news. "He was elderly, though. I hope he went quickly and without pain."

"He went in his sleep."

"That's good."

Helen led Harper and Jared to a small kitchen table and poured mugs of coffee for each before settling. If she thought it weird that two people were asking questions about a fire from more than two decades before, she didn't let on. "So … how can I help you?"

"Well, we've had an … incident," Jared explained, leaning back in his chair and giving off a friendly vibe. "Arthur's widow came into the police department several days ago. She had photographs of a body."

"Oh, my!" Helen's hand flew to her mouth. "That's terrible."

"We searched her home and found nothing in the general vicinity of where she found the photos, but upon a search of the grounds we discovered a body in the woods behind the house," Jared continued. "The body has been there for some time and the medical examiner is trying to pin down a cause of death."

"And you think Arthur killed this person?"

"I think that there were photos of a dead woman in the attic and a body on the property," Jared clarified. He didn't believe he would get anywhere by talking smack to Helen about the man who saved her life. "We're just trying to get answers."

"Well, I don't know what to tell you about the fire," Helen said. "I woke up in the middle of the night to a bunch of smoke. My eyes burned and I could hear my son crying. I tried to get to him, but it was difficult and then Arthur appeared out of nowhere and helped us out of the house."

"Do you know what started the fire?"

"Faulty wiring on a slow cooker," Helen replied. "The fire inspector said it was a fluke. The insurance covered everything – which was good – but we lost a lot of family mementos. Without Arthur, though, I'm not sure if I would've been able to find my son in all of that smoke. I'm not proud of it, but I was starting to panic when he appeared out of nowhere."

"I don't blame you," Harper said, her eyes flashing with sympathy. "Did you get to know Arthur after that?"

"He honestly seemed embarrassed by all of the attention," Helen replied. "Everyone kept calling him a hero and he didn't like it. He got grouchy with anyone who even mentioned it."

"As far as I could tell he was grouchy with everyone," Harper intoned.

"Only on the surface," Helen said, a small smile playing at the corners of her mouth. "He was kind of a misunderstood man, if you ask me. He wasn't happy, there's no getting around that. He had a kind heart, though. He bought me a brand new slow cooker once I got a new place."

"That's kind of sweet," Harper said. "Or ... kind of weird given how your fire started."

"Yeah, I thought it was weird, too," Helen admitted. "He didn't do it out of malice, though. I still have that slow cooker somewhere. I never wanted to use one again after the fire, but I couldn't throw it away because it was from him."

"Then I guess it was definitely sweet," Jared said, using both of his hands to cup the coffee mug. "You said the fire was in the middle of the night. What time?"

"It was well after midnight," Helen said. "I'd put a roast in the slow cooker on low overnight so we could eat it the next day. I was in bed a good hour before I woke up. I think it was actually closer to two."

"Did Arthur say what he was doing in your neck of the woods at two in the morning?"

Helen stilled, surprised. "You know, I never asked that question. I was just happy he was there. Maybe he was visiting my neighbor. Although ... if he was, I never saw him there before or after. I'm pretty sure he didn't know her, now that I think about it. I would've heard about that."

"Who was your neighbor?"

"Tess Hilliard."

Harper and Jared exchanged a weighted look.

"I see," Jared said, forcing a smile. "You've been a great help. Thank you so much for your time."

Thirteen

"That can't be a coincidence, right?" Harper was animated during the drive back to Whisper Cove and Jared couldn't help but be relieved that she seemed to be putting her fight with Zander behind her ... er, well, at least for now.

"I think the odds of that being a coincidence would have to be astronomical," Jared said, checking his rearview mirror before turning onto the main road that led through the heart of Whisper Cove. "I mean ... Tess lived next door to a woman Arthur saved from a fire in the middle of the night. Her body was found on his property."

"Plus when you add the photos ... ."

"Exactly." Jared grabbed Harper's hand as he drove, rubbing his thumb over her knuckles as he mulled over various possibilities. "All we're missing is a motive."

"Are we?" Harper wasn't convinced. "Maybe Tess was pressuring Arthur to leave Annette and marry her. Maybe Tess threatened to tell Annette."

"Okay, for the sake of argument, let's say you're right," Jared said. "Arthur would've been much older than Tess. She was forty when she died, which would've made him about sixty-five at the time."

"Apparently age means nothing for perverts."

"Yes, I'm hopeful that's true for me, too."

Harper graced him with a rueful smile as she shook her head. "Are you planning on being a dirty old man?"

"Only if you're around to wash me in the bathtub on a regular basis."

Harper lowered her eyes as warmth spread throughout her chest. "You're already thinking of growing old with me?" It was a bold question and she wasn't sure if she wanted to press him for an answer.

"Yup."

"That's kind of … ."

"Cute?"

"Sexy."

"I'll take it." Jared graced Harper with a small smile before returning to business. "By the time Arthur would've hooked up with Annette, his children would've been grown and out of the house."

"I believe they had three of them. Two girls and a boy."

"Still, if Arthur was in love with Tess, there's no reason he wouldn't leave his wife," Jared pointed out. "There was no reason to stay together for the sake of the family."

"You're assuming Arthur was in love with Tess," Harper pointed out. "That might not be the case. He was an older guy and Tess apparently slept with everyone because she was hoping to hook a big fish. Arthur might've only been in it for the sex, and if Tess pressured him for more than he was willing to give … ."

"Then he might've snapped," Jared surmised. "Still, by every account we've heard, Arthur and Annette hated each other. She probably would've been fine with him stepping out as long as it was under the radar."

"I think that's assuming facts not in evidence."

"Do tell, my sexy lawyer."

"I'm just saying that I've known Annette for a lot of years," Harper said, her lips twitching. "She's always been very … proprietary."

"Give me an example."

"Okay, they had a gardener for years when I was a kid," Harper explained. "His name was Benny and he was friends with my dad. He did all of their landscaping. He also cultivated some sort of rare rose on her property and then entered it in a fair."

"I have no idea what you're saying."

"I'm getting there," Harper chastised. "Give me a moment. Anyway, Benny won first prize – which essentially amounted to no money and a blue ribbon – and Annette was so furious when she found out that he used one of her roses that she demanded the newspaper print a correction and name her the winner."

"Even though he's the one who tended the roses."

"Exactly," Harper said, leaning forward as she warmed to her subject. "I don't think Annette was ever the type of woman who would look the other way during an ongoing affair. She might not have wanted Arthur, but I'm guessing she didn't want anyone else to have him either."

"So we're back to the first theory," Jared said. "Arthur was looking to dip his wick, he picked the town's favorite date, and she did something that irritated him enough that she ended up dead."

"We really need to find someone who was close to Tess before she died," Harper said. "We have no idea what she was thinking at the time of her death. This is all conjecture."

"Mel is trying to track down Tess's sister. She used to live in the area. We're hopeful she hasn't moved too far away."

"So what is the plan now?" Harper asked, shifting her eyes to the thick trees on either side of Annette's driveway as Jared directed his vehicle toward the house. "Are you going to tell Annette what we know?"

"I'm going to feel her out," Jared clarified. "I don't want to upset her – mostly because I'm worried she could stab me through the heart with a knitting needle if I'm not careful – but we need some information. Let's just play it by ear."

"That sounds like a plan."

"WHO ARE you?"

The man who opened the door of Annette's house furrowed his brow when his gaze landed on Harper and Jared.

"I'm Jared Monroe. This is Harper Harlow. I … we're here to see Mrs. Fleming."

"I'm her son. May I ask what this is pertaining to?"

"The body found at the back of the property."

"Oh." The man looked thoughtful for a moment and then shook his head. "I'm sorry. I'm Matthew Fleming. You're the police officer who discovered the body? Mother mentioned it and I saw something brief on the news, but I thought she was exaggerating."

"Exaggerating?" Harper had a hard time believing that.

"Forgive me," Matthew said, pushing open the door and ushering them inside. "I guess you probably want an explanation. It's been a difficult few months and this recent *development* only adds to the stress."

"Okay, fill us in," Jared said, taking a seat on the flowered couch in the living room as Matthew settled in a chair. "Just out of curiosity's sake, though, where is your mother?"

"She's taking a nap in the drawing room," Matthew replied. "Er, well, she calls it a 'drawing room.' It's really just a small den with a television. She was watching one of her stories and fell asleep. I closed the door so I wouldn't wake her."

"That's nice, but we kind of need to talk to her," Jared hedged.

"Let me explain a few things and then I'll wake her. Will that work?"

Jared nodded as he leaned back on the sofa. It was older, the upholstery something out of the 1970s if he had to guess, but it wasn't altogether uncomfortable. "Sure. What's on your mind?"

"I live in Grand Rapids," Matthew explained. "I just arrived this morning after receiving a call from my mother. I haven't lived in Whisper Cove in almost thirty years."

Harper pursed her lips. That meant Matthew was long gone before Arthur took up with Tess. She couldn't help but wonder if he knew about his father's wandering eye.

"Okay," Jared said. "Is there a reason you're here now? Other than the obvious, I mean."

"My mother has always been strong-willed and stubborn," Matthew replied. "I've been trying to get her to move near me ever since my father died. I wasn't as worried about her when he was still around, but she's been … uncooperative … whenever I bring up the suggestion."

Harper couldn't help but smirk. "I'll bet."

"Harper Harlow." Matthew rolled the name through his head. "Is your father Phil Harlow?"

"He is."

"Phil and I went to school together. How is he?"

"The same."

"That's good," Matthew said. "You remind me of him a bit. It must be the eyes."

"It must be."

"Anyway, my mother called me several days ago to say she found photographs depicting a dead body in the attic," Matthew supplied. "I thought she was … exaggerating."

"Does your mother often make up stories?" Jared asked.

"Not 'make up,'" Matthew clarified. "She doesn't do anything out of malice. She merely gets confused."

"That's part of the aging process," Harper said helpfully. "She seems pretty on top of things from what I can tell."

"Yes and no," Matthew countered. "She has good days and bad days. On good days she's exactly like the mother I remember – which is to say she's a difficult woman who I manage to love despite the way she picks at me.

"On a bad day, though, she seems to get lost in time or wander around for hours on end not knowing who she is," he continued. "I was hoping it would pass, or perhaps even level out, but that doesn't seem likely."

"Has she been diagnosed?" Jared asked.

"She has dementia," Matthew answered. "She's fairly lucky to have staved it off for as long as she did given her age, but she's only going to get worse now. She won't get better."

"I'm so sorry to hear that," Harper said, sympathy overwhelming her. "What are you going to do?"

"I'm going to move my mother into an assisted living center close to me," Matthew replied. "In fact, my wife is there securing a room even as we speak. I took two weeks of vacation to help my mother sort through everything in the house."

Something occurred to Jared. "Does she know that? I'm going to be honest, she hasn't been acting like a woman who will be leaving her home soon. In fact, she said she was cleaning out the attic because she wanted to go through your father's junk and get rid of it. She didn't mention anything about packing or moving."

"There have been ongoing discussions, but she refuses to listen to reason," Matthew said. "I'm afraid she doesn't have much of a choice. She is unable to live on her own. I would like to take her into my home, but she hates my wife and I've been threatened with a divorce if I even consider it. The assisted living center is only two blocks away and she can leave for day visits so … it really is the best I can swing given the circumstances."

"It doesn't sound so bad," Harper said, flashing a smile. "She's not going to want to leave her home, though."

"I understand that. There's no one here to help her, though. I can't give her everything she wants because it's simply impossible."

"You said she called you about the photographs," Jared prodded. "You didn't believe her?"

"I thought she might've come across some of my father's old stash of Playboys or something and been confused," Matthew admitted. "They were stashed all over the house. I used to steal them when I was a teenager."

"I think that's a normal rite of passage," Jared said, smiling. "The photos are real, though. She brought them into the police station. That's how Harper and I ended up out here. We searched the attic and came up empty. It was so hot up there we decided to take a break and get some air.

"We walked by the river and that's when we saw the hand poking out of the ground," he continued. "The medical examiner believes that flooding eroded the soil. The body has been there for twenty-five years. The woman in the grave has been identified as Tess Hilliard. Does that name ring any bells for you?"

Matthew tilted his head to the side, his mind clearly busy. "I'm sorry. I can't say that it does."

"She was forty at the time of her death," Harper said. "She lived out on Eastland Road. Not long before she disappeared, Tess's neighbor had a fire. Your father saved that neighbor and her son."

"I remember that," Matthew said. "Everyone thought he was a hero and he was strangely silent on the topic."

"Why do you say it like that?" Jared asked.

"Because my father was the type of person who liked to take credit for things he didn't do," Matthew replied. "I couldn't figure out why he wanted to forget the one heroic thing he really did do.

"Look, I loved my father a great deal, but pretending he wasn't difficult to live with would be a lie," he continued. "I love my mother, too, before you ask. She's just ... persnickety. Of course, that's kind of a nice word to use. She's also mean when she wants to be."

"I don't want to offend you, but I'm going to go for broke here," Jared said. "We have reason to believe that your father might've been having an affair with Tess Hilliard. Perhaps she pressured him to leave your mother, or maybe even threatened to out him if he didn't give in to a specific demand or something, but the working theory is that he killed her to keep her quiet."

"If you expect me to be shocked by your assertion, I'm not," Matthew said. "I believe my father was capable of murder, although I would imagine it would more likely happen with a gun and a fifth of whiskey close by than whatever you're describing. I honestly don't ever remember hearing that woman's name before, though.

"As for having an affair, I'm not sure that was in his wheelhouse," he continued. "He and my mother were far from happy, but he didn't seem interested in wandering to other women as much as he seemed to delight in ignoring my mother.

"If you say he had an affair with this woman, I have no reason not to believe you," he said. "I just can't see it for some reason. That doesn't sound a thing like him."

Jared exchanged a quick look with Harper and nodded before pushing himself to a standing position. "Okay, well, thank you for your time." He extended his hand so Matthew could shake it. "We'll still want to talk to your mother, but we won't bother her right this second. I'll have my partner Mel Kelsey swing by later. She knows him better and he can ask the same questions I would."

"That would be great," Matthew said. "In the meantime, I'll keep track of her moods and keep my eyes open as I sort through the items in the house. We're going to be separating everything for an estate sale, so no stone will be left unturned under this roof. I promise you that."

"Thank you. Let us know if you come up with something."

FOURTEEN

"What did Mel say?"

Harper shifted until she was comfortable in the passenger seat of Jared's cruiser, her body protesting against another long drive. She wasn't used to spending so much time in a vehicle, but she had no intention of complaining. As far as she was concerned, Jared was saving her from an uncomfortable day at the office with Zander. He was a hero, quite frankly, and she much preferred an aching back to Zander's snark.

"He found Tess's sister," Jared replied, turning onto the highway. "She's in Washington Township."

"Oh, that's not too far away." Harper was secretly relieved.

"I see you squirming over there," Jared teased. "Is your back bothering you?"

"Let's just say you're going to owe me the best massage ever later."

"Is that before or after you rub the heck out of me?"

"I … haven't decided yet."

Jared chuckled at the adorable look on her face and shook his head. Despite her crazy shenanigans of late, he enjoyed spending time with her. She was always smart and fast on her feet, and he liked the fact that he could be himself without having to constantly worry that he would say something to inadvertently offend her. She was pretty easygoing … as long as you weren't her best friend and tried to keep something from her.

"The sister is expecting us," Jared said. "She seemed surprised by the call, but she's willing to talk to us."

"Did Mel say why she was so hard to track down? I mean ... she's not very far away. We should've been able to find her in the records that first day."

"She's been married three times since then," Jared supplied. "I get the feeling that the Hilliard family has a genetic fickle bone or something."

"Ha, ha."

"I don't know why we're just getting to her now," Jared said after a beat. "It simply took a bit of effort to track her down. Mel made notification and then said we would be coming out to talk to her. He was willing to do it, but I asked him to sit down with Annette instead."

"What do you think about that?" Harper was genuinely curious. "Do you think she knew about Tess?"

"I have no idea. If the son didn't know, I think there's a good chance that Annette didn't know. Of course, Annette remained in town and Whisper Cove is fat with gossip so the odds of her not knowing if other people did seem slim."

"I don't understand why people cheat." Harper stared out the window, her eyes trained on the blurring foliage as the vehicle whizzed by. "If you're unhappy with someone, why not get divorced?"

"I think in some cases that people shouldn't get married at all," Jared countered. "If you love someone, it's easy not to cheat. The problem comes when two people unite when they probably shouldn't do it because they're not really devoted to one another."

"Have you ever cheated on anyone?"

"Just on a math test when I was in eighth grade. I felt so guilty I spilled my guts to my father and he marched me into the principal's office and made me confess. I had detention for a month."

"That's not really what I was talking about."

"I know," Jared said, grinning. "I have never cheated. I've never had the inclination. If I don't like someone, I don't continue dating them."

Harper seemed happy with the answer and the couple lapsed into amiable silence. After a few minutes, though, she slid her eyes back in his direction and tilted her head to the side, causing her blond hair to cascade past her shoulders. "How come you didn't ask if I've ever cheated?"

Jared barked out a laugh. "Because I know you. You're not a cheater. You're so loyal that you've spent days pouting about Zander hiding a secret."

"You don't know," Harper argued. "I could've been a total bad girl at some point in my life. I could've had eight boyfriends at once."

"You don't have it in you. You're too loyal. You're a good girl."

"I'm pretty sure you meant that as an insult."

"I'm pretty sure you're my favorite person in the world and I would never purposely insult you." Jared lifted their linked hands and pressed a kiss to her knuckles. "While we're on the subject, though, when are you going to forgive Zander?"

"In two years."

"Two years?"

"That's how mad I am at him."

"Do you want to hear what I think?"

"Not even a little bit."

Jared heaved out a heavy sigh. "I'm going to tell you anyway," he said, ignoring the dirty look she tossed in his direction. "I don't think you're angry. I think you're hurt."

"I am not hurt."

"Yes, you are." Jared was firm and refused to back down. "You think Zander is lying to you because of something you did. I think you need to consider the possibility that Zander didn't tell you because he was confused."

"Confused about what?"

"The fact that he couldn't find anything wrong with Shawn."

"But … that makes absolutely no sense."

"Heart, you and Zander have been everything to each other for so long that you've built up a wall that's almost impossible to penetrate," Jared said. "Think about it. The only reason you let me in was because you were feeling vulnerable at the time. Another day … another ghost … I might not have been welcome in your life."

"That is preposterous." Harper turned so her shoulders were squared as she stared down Jared. "I let you in because my heart wanted it. I felt something when I met you. I can't explain it. You always would've been welcome in my life."

"That's nice, but I still think that Zander is dealing with something new and you should give him a break," Jared said. "He always finds something wrong with the guys he dates. He never goes on a second date. We both knew he'd eventually find someone he really connected with. Isn't there a possibility – even a small one – that he simply panicked when he couldn't find an errant body hair?"

Harper didn't want to smile, but she couldn't help herself. "I guess it's a possibility," she conceded. "He still lied to me."

"And you guys have to work that out. While you're figuring out how to do that, though, remember that he's always been the one person who has your back no matter the circumstances."

Harper's eyes glistened with tears as she nodded, quickly turning her head toward the door to hide the overflowing emotion. "How come you're suddenly on his side?"

"Because I want this to work for all of us. I think Shawn's presence could be a good thing for everybody. This is never going to work out if you and he can't find some solid ground, though. I don't want my heart to break so you and Zander need to make up."

"I would never break your heart."

"Not on purpose, but if Zander breaks yours you might not be able to stop yourself." Jared squeezed her hand, drawing her eyes back to him. "Just think about it. That's all I ask."

MADISON TELLER met Harper and Jared at the door, exchanging a series of lame pleasantries before showing them into her house and offering them a spot of tea. Once everyone was settled, she wasted no time asking questions.

"How did my sister die?"

"We don't know." Jared felt pity for the woman, but he could do nothing but tell the truth. "Her body was completely bones when we found it. The medical examiner is still going over the evidence. Without flesh … well … sometimes it's hard to determine the manner of death."

"But you're sure she was murdered?"

"I guess we can't say that we're absolutely sure," Jared conceded. "There was blood in the photographs, though, and someone went to a lot of trouble to bury a body if it was an accident."

"I guess that makes sense." Madison gripped her hands together on her lap as she shifted uncomfortably on her chair. "Do you know who did it?"

"We're looking at a few leads," Jared replied. "Her body was found on a parcel of property owned by Arthur Fleming. Does that name mean anything to you?"

"He was one of Tess's boyfriends." Madison twisted her face to show her disgust. "He was a mean and nasty guy, but that didn't stop Tess from sleeping with him. That didn't stop Tess from sleeping with any of them. She had freaking tragic taste in men."

Jared lifted his eyebrows, surprised by the woman's bluntness. "How long did Tess and Arthur date?"

"I don't think you could call what they did dating. Tess met men by the bushel at that bar where she used to work. She had pie-in-the-sky dreams, my sister. She thought she was going to eventually stumble across the right one and he was going to take her out of Whisper Cove and give her the life she always wanted."

"That wasn't really an answer," Jared pointed out.

"Oh, well, I believe Arthur and Tess had relations for about a year," Madison said. "It was all very hush-hush. Arthur used to go to the bar once a week to play cards with his friends and it started out as pure flirting. I mean … the man was twenty-five years older than Tess. It wasn't a love match right out of the gate."

"Did that bother her?"

"She didn't care about that. She didn't care about age or looks. She cared about money and what people could offer her. She took one look at that big house Arthur shared with his wife and thought there was a chance she might end up in it."

Harper widened her eyes, surprised. "But … how? Surely she didn't think Annette was going to just roll over and hand that house to her."

"I don't think she even considered Annette," Madison said. "I loved my sister. She was my best friend. She didn't, however, have a great set of morals on her. Mind you, we all make mistakes, but my sister kept making the same ones over and over again.

"All Tess could see was that house," she continued. "That's why she purposely got pregnant. She was trying to trap Arthur so he had no choice but to leave Annette and make an honest woman of her."

Jared's stomach flipped. "Pregnant? She was pregnant with Arthur's baby?"

"She gave birth to Arthur's baby," Madison clarified. "It was about three months before her disappearance."

Harper was flabbergasted. "Did anyone know she was pregnant?"

"She didn't get huge or anything, but I reckon everyone who ran in her circle knew that she was pregnant," Madison replied. "She thought that baby was going to solve all of her problems. Joshua. She thought Joshua was going to be the pot of gold at the end of her rainbow."

"I'm sorry, I don't understand," Jared said, gripping his knees as he rested the palms of his hands against the knobby surfaces. "I didn't see any mention of a child in any of Tess's records. Are you sure she had a baby?"

Madison snorted, amused. "I'm sure." She pointed to a photograph on the wall, a handsome young man with dark hair and eyes smiling back. "That's him. I raised him as my own."

"Did you adopt him?"

Madison nodded. "I knew my sister was dead," she explained. "The cops said she ran off, but I knew that she wouldn't leave Joshua. It wasn't out of some misguided sense of motherhood, mind you, but she wasn't done trying to leverage him against Arthur. She had a plan for getting what she wanted."

"Why didn't you tell the police this when your sister went missing?" Harper asked. "Surely they would've investigated given this information."

"I did tell the police. Scotty Walker was the chief back then. He said Tess had a reputation and he wasn't hauling Arthur in for questioning on the strength of gossip."

"I'm sorry," Jared said, shaking his head. He felt sick to his stomach. "That never should've happened."

"It doesn't matter now," Madison said, her eyes kind. "I knew Tess was dead. I knew Arthur probably did it, but he's dead now, too. I raised Joshua and he's been a true joy. I'm the only mother he has ever known."

"Does he know about Tess?" Harper couldn't stop herself from asking the question.

"He does." Madison bobbed her head. "He asked a lot of questions when he was a teenager, but if he's still curious, he keeps it to himself. He graduated with honors from the University of Michigan. He got a full scholarship.

He got a job as an engineer at Ford right after graduation." Madison's pride was evident.

"It sounds as if you gave him the best possible world to grow up in," Harper said, admiration rolling off of her. "You did what your sister couldn't."

"I did what had to be done. You take care of family."

"You're still amazing."

Madison smiled at Harper before sobering and focusing on Jared. "So what happens now?"

"If Arthur is a killer – and that's definitely looking to be the case – there isn't a lot we can do," Jared replied. "We'll try to close the case through official channels and give you some closure."

"What about Arthur's wife?"

"She has dementia and will be moving to a home in Grand Rapids in a few weeks."

"Does she know about Tess?"

"My partner is interviewing her now, but I don't think so," Jared replied. "His son didn't know."

"Matthew?" Madison furrowed her brow. "He was a youngster back then. Tess said she had a mind to go after him if Arthur wouldn't give her what she wanted. She was petty like that. Thankfully she never got the chance."

"Yes, well, I'm not sure what to make of that so I'm just going to file it away to think about later," Jared said, getting to his feet. "Thank you so much for your time and being so honest. We'll be in touch as soon as we have more information."

"Thank you." Madison walked Harper and Jared to the door, only speaking again when they were on the other side of the threshold. "If you can get any justice for Tess, I would appreciate it. Even though he would never say it, I think it would mean something to Joshua. It's better to have a mother taken than willingly walk away."

"We'll do our best," Jared said. "I'll have the medical examiner get in touch with you. He'll ask where you want the remains sent when he's done examining them."

Madison blew out a sigh. "A funeral. It seems kind of weird to be planning it now when she died so long ago. Still, Tess was a good woman who made bad decisions. She deserves a proper goodbye."

"We'll be in touch," Jared said. "If you think of anything else, don't hesitate to give me a call."

FIFTEEN

"I put my bag in your bedroom. I hope that's all right."

Harper smiled as she rounded the main hallway corner in Jared's rental home later that night, pulling up short when she caught sight of the blanket resting in the center of the hardwood floor. While she'd been in the other room unpacking her overnight bag, Jared lit a multitude of candles and placed them around the room. He'd also put the takeout subs they bought at the area pizza shop on plates and placed them in the center of the blanket.

"What's this?"

"It's a picnic," Jared replied, smirking. "It's better than a normal picnic, though, because we don't have to contend with bugs."

"Oh, this is so sweet." Harper pressed her lips together as she shuffled closer, her eyes glistening in the muted light. "I can't believe you did this."

"I put a blanket on the floor and grabbed five candles," Jared clarified. "I hardly think that qualifies me for sainthood."

"Especially knowing what a sinner you're going to be later tonight," Harper teased, taking Jared's hand as she eased onto the blanket and got comfortable next to him. "It's still really sweet."

"We haven't had a chance to be alone very often over the past few weeks, so I thought I would take advantage of the opportunity."

"We've been alone like five nights in a row thanks to Zander and his lying tongue."

Jared pursed his lips, his expression unreadable as he studied Harper's angular face. She was a breathtaking woman, but it wasn't her face stealing his patience and heart this evening. "We need to talk."

Harper's shoulders stiffened as she shifted her eyes to Jared. Fear flitted through her and for a moment she couldn't help but wonder if she'd pushed things too far. "I … ."

"Wipe that look off your face," Jared chided, wagging a finger for emphasis. "I know exactly what you're thinking and it bugs me."

Harper recovered quickly. "Maybe you bug me."

"I don't think there's any 'maybe' about it. We're still going to talk."

Harper exhaled heavily. "Is this the part where you tell me I'm being unreasonable and need to grow up?"

"Yes."

She was expecting the succinct answer, but it still hurt. "Wow. Don't hold back."

"If I thought holding back would help you, that's exactly what I would do." Jared rolled so he sat with his knees raised and his elbows resting across them. "I've only known you for a few months, but I'd like to believe I understand you. I'd like to believe that I'm someone you can confide in and rely on."

"You are," Harper said, her temper flaring. "How can you doubt that?"

"Because the last few days have been all about you," Jared answered, opting for bluntness over style. "We've spent a lot of time together – which I really enjoy – but you've been so fixated on Zander that it's felt more like work than a relationship."

Harper snapped a hand to her mouth, horrified. "What?"

"I need you not to freak out," Jared cautioned, resting his hand on her knee to offer reassurance. "I am not angry. I knew when I got involved with you that there was going to be Zander drama from time to time. I think my mistake was assuming that it was always going to be him providing the drama.

"Close your mouth right now and let me finish, Heart," he continued. "You've been a freaking handful the past few days, and it hasn't been enjoyable to watch. Before you do some weird chick thing and assume that means I want to break up or storm out in a huff, I think I've earned a bit of leeway here.

"You and Zander are dramatic and enjoyable and I love hanging out with both of you, but I sometimes feel that I'm the third wheel in this relationship," he said. "You seem to be ignoring what I need and want and focusing on Zander to the detriment of all else. I don't want that to continue."

Harper sat in silence for a moment, her blue eyes cloudy. "Are you done?"

"For now." Jared braced himself for a verbal attack. "Let me have it."

Harper swallowed hard as she tilted her head to the side and stared at one of the candles. She focused on the flame so hard the orange edges blurred as her heart rolled with pity and anger. The anger wasn't at Jared, though. It was at herself.

"I'm sorry."

Jared's eyebrows winged up his forehead. "You're sorry? I expected you to explode all over me."

"How can I do that when you're right?" Harper asked, leveling her gaze on Jared's handsome face. "Even when I know I'm going overboard with Zander sometimes I can't seem to help myself. Ever since we hooked up as a couple, Jared, I've been going out of my way to make sure he doesn't feel left out.

"I know you may not understand it – and you've been unbelievably kind and patient given the way Zander and I interact with one another – but he is the only person who has always been there for me and I feel a certain sense of … obligation … where he's concerned," she continued. "When I was little everyone thought I needed professional help because I thought I could see ghosts. Zander never thought that. He was the only one. Even my parents didn't believe me."

Jared silently captured Harper's hand and pressed it to his chest as he listened. He was ready for her to unburden herself.

"Even after my parents started believing, everyone thought I was weird and I had very few friends," Harper continued. "Zander was always there, though. He never left me. He could've gone to any college he wanted and yet he chose to go with me. I think he was worried I wouldn't make friends without him.

"After the Quinn situation – Zander really never liked him as much as he does you, for the record – Zander closed ranks around me because everyone thought I was crazy for going out into the woods and searching for him," she continued. "I had to, though. I had to know. Not knowing is worse than knowing.

"He's the one person who has always been steady and constant in my life – even when he's unsteady that's somehow still steady because I know to expect it," she said.

"I didn't mean to favor him over you. I honestly didn't. I just didn't want him to feel left out."

"And I'm okay with that," Jared said, slipping his hand to the back of her neck so he could rub out the tension. "Harper, I'm well aware that Zander isn't going anywhere. I need you to focus on the fact that he wasn't trying to hurt you when he didn't tell you about Shawn. He was trying to figure things out on his own."

"It still hurts."

Jared couldn't help but smile at the stubborn tilt of her head. "I'm sure it does," he conceded. "This could be good for all of us, though. You don't want Zander to be alone and you've spent years worrying he would never find someone he can spend more than a night with.

"Shawn seems steady and agreeable and I'm totally going to run a background check on him to make sure he's not a murderer," he continued, his lips twitching. "Zander needs someone to love. You guys cannot be everything to each other any longer. There are other people involved. That's okay. That's how it's supposed to go."

"But ... what happens now?" Harper's eyes flooded with emotion. "If Zander has Shawn, he's not going to need me."

"Did you stop needing Zander when you got me?"

"No."

"Then why do you assume the reverse is true?"

"I ... don't know." Harper rubbed her cheek, misery clinging to her features. "He's the best friend I've ever had."

"And part of your heart will always be untouchable to me because it belongs to him," Jared said. "I'm okay with that as long as the rest of your heart is open to me. Zander deserves to be loved by someone who can give him the things you can't – and before you ask me about that, no, I won't go into detail."

Harper giggled. "You really like Shawn, don't you?"

"I do. He's even-tempered and seems fine with Zander's mood swings. He barely blinked at the display you two put on over dinner last night … and again this morning."

"So you think I should talk to Zander."

"I think you should eat your dinner and then hop into bed with me," Jared corrected. "Then, after a good night's sleep, I think you should make up with Zander. This arrangement could be great for all of us, Harper. It eases a lot of the strife in the house."

"Strife? Good word."

"Zander used it the other day when discussing why white pants should never be worn by men. I believe the intent is that he would have strife with anyone who would dare do it."

"Ah."

Jared pressed a soft kiss to Harper's cheek, thankful she turned into him instead of pulling away. "I want this to work out for everyone, but you have to let go of Zander a little bit. Not a lot, mind you, but a little bit is necessary. If you guys can relax and let Shawn and me in, we're all going to be a lot happier."

Harper was silent for so long Jared worried he'd lost her. When she finally opened her mouth, she seemed to be in better control. "Does this mean you're going to rub me once we get in bed so I can relax? I mean, that is the goal, right?"

Jared grinned, amused. "Yes."

"I guess I can live with that."

Jared smacked a loud kiss against the corner of her mouth. "I think we all can. It's going to be okay. I promise. Now ... eat your sub. I'm going to be ready to move this picnic to a new location in exactly ten minutes ... so chew fast."

"And they say romance is dead."

JARED dropped Harper off at her house early the next morning before pointing himself toward the police station. He considered offering to venture inside with her – thinking perhaps his presence would ease the tension – but in the end he decided Harper and Zander had to do this themselves. They would be stronger for it when they came out the other side.

Harper was nervous as she slipped her key into the door, and when she pushed it open she found herself staring at Shawn instead of Zander. The man sat on the couch, a mug of coffee warming in his hands, and he seemed intent on the morning news. When he shifted his eyes to Harper, he flashed a welcoming smile even as a flash of nervous energy flitted across his features.

"Good morning."

"Good morning," Harper murmured, sucking in a breath as she squared her shoulders. "How are you today?"

"I'm good." Shawn looked uncomfortable as he moved his legs out of Harper's path so she could drop her bag on the other side of the couch. "Did you have a good night with Jared?"

"Yeah. He made a picnic on the floor. It had candles and everything."

"That sounds romantic."

"He also told me to suck it up and make up with Zander." Harper had no idea why she admitted that to

Shawn, but she was almost relieved when the words escaped her mouth. Perhaps it was a test. Perhaps it was a way to regain superiority in her own house. Or perhaps it was simply nice to be able to confide in someone who understood what a pain Zander could be when pushed into a corner. "He thinks I'm being unreasonable."

"What do you think?" Shawn kept his face blank as he sipped his coffee.

"I think I was hurt because Zander kept you from me. I think that made me mean and irrational. I think Jared is a saint for putting up with my moods these past few days. I also think I owe Zander an apology ... but he owes me one, too."

Shawn pursed his lips, his eyes dancing as they skimmed over Harper. "I think that sounds fair. He's in the kitchen cooking breakfast."

"So I should probably go in there." Harper said the words but remained rooted to her spot as she stared at the open archway.

"He's not going to pick a fight," Shawn offered. "He wants to make up with you as much as you want to make up with him. He tossed and turned ... and mercilessly complained ... all night. He's very unhappy. I can't say for certain why he didn't tell you – it's not my place – but I think it might've been fear. It certainly wasn't a personal dig at you."

"I know all about that," Harper said, her smile rueful. "I'm going to go in there now. If you hear things being thrown or screaming, don't be alarmed. That's normal."

"I'm just going to watch the news. You guys do what you need to do."

Harper shuffled toward the archway, her eyes appraising as they looked Shawn up and down. His hair was rumpled from sleep, but he looked completely comfortable in their living room. Heck, he looked as if he belonged there.

"Jared says I'm going to like you," Harper said. "I think he's right."

Shawn's smile was earnest. "I know I'm going to like you."

Harper smiled to herself as she moved toward the kitchen, girding herself for an emotional battle. She'd been mentally preparing herself for this all night. She didn't expect it to be easy.

Zander glanced up from the counter island where he mixed pancake batter. He registered surprise when he saw Harper instead of Shawn. "I didn't know you were back."

"Jared just dropped me off."

"Oh."

The silence was uncomfortable and foreign to both of them. Zander was the first to break it.

"Did you have a good time?"

Harper bit her lip and nodded. "We had a picnic."

"That sounds fun."

"Jared also told me I'm being unreasonable and should apologize to you."

Zander froze at the words. "What do you think?"

"I think I love you and I'm sorry." The words easily escaped and Harper felt lighter once they did. "I'm still hurt that you didn't tell me what was happening, but nothing will ever change how much I love you."

A lone tear slid down Zander's cheek as he shifted his eyes to her. "I love you, too, Harp. I'm sorry I didn't tell you. It just kind of spiraled out of hand from the beginning. It took me by surprise."

"It's okay."

"It's not okay, but … we'll make it okay." Zander's hands were shaky as he left the spoon in the pancake batter and edged around the counter. Harper was already hurrying to him before he even opened his arms.

The duo made a loud "oomph" sound as they collided, tears mingling and arms flailing as they hugged one another.

"I'm so sorry," Harper gasped. "I didn't mean what I said."

"I didn't either. I'm sorry, too."

For a few moments all that could be heard was sniffling. Then Shawn appeared in the doorway and graced them both with a wide smile. "Who wants breakfast? I think it will be a great 'get to know you' meal."

And just like that, the storm passed.

"That sounds great," Harper said, stepping away as she wiped an errant tear from her cheek. "I want bacon, too."

"A girl after my own heart," Shawn teased.

"A girl after both our hearts," Zander corrected. "Pancakes and bacon it is. If there ever was a time to forget my diet, this is it. Bring on the carbs and grease. I don't even care if I can't wear a bathing suit this week."

"Oh, it's a summer miracle," Harper intoned, giggling when Zander poked her side. "Happy summer, one and all."

SIXTEEN

"I thought you forgot about me."

Janet Markowitz was surly on a good day. The expression on her face told Zander and Harper that she was going to be something else entirely when they parked next to the barn shortly after breakfast.

"We could never forget about you," Zander cooed, his expression reflecting feigned delight as he grabbed a box from the back seat of his car. "You're the reason we live and breathe."

Janet knit her eyebrows together as she looked Zander up and down. "Do you think I don't know what sarcasm is?"

"I wasn't being sarcastic."

"You're the king of sarcasm," Janet shot back, rolling her eyes. "I called your office yesterday, by the way, and your assistant – the one with the stupid hair – said that you guys were off dealing with an important business matter."

"I think Molly's hair is delightful," Harper countered. "I wish I could pull off the color. Cool tones wash me out."

"They do not," Zander scoffed. "You look great in blues and purples. It's red that makes you look idiotic. Remember when you decided you just had to have that red wool coat that one year? You looked like a walking tomato."

The corners of Harper's mouth tipped down. "That was a very nice jacket. It was designer. I loved that jacket." Until she didn't. After wearing the jacket out, Harper found she couldn't wear red again. She simply grew to hate the color. She refused to admit that to Zander, though.

"It was ugly."

"You're ugly."

"I happen to be the handsomest man in the world," Zander said, puffing out his chest. "Men will write songs about me one day."

Despite the feigned argument, Harper couldn't hide the sloppy smile sliding across her face. "I really missed you."

Zander tugged on a strand of her flaxen hair and matched the smile. "I missed you more."

"Oh, geez." Janet made an exaggerated face as she rolled her eyes. "I get it. You two are gooey and in love again. You were fighting the other day and now you want to hop in each other's britches. Can you delay that until you deal with my ghost?"

"We're best friends," Harper supplied. "We don't date."

"I thought you lived together."

"As best friends."

"I will never understand the youth of today," Janet muttered, annoyed. "You've got things screwed up. You're not supposed to live with a man until you marry him."

"What if the man is just a friend and you don't feel romantic about each other?" Harper pressed. "What's wrong with that?" She found she enjoyed messing with Janet. The woman had a puritan stance that was downright adorable.

"I don't believe men and women can be friends. There's always sex."

"Not between us," Zander said, tilting his head to the side when he heard something crash inside the barn. Apparently the poltergeist was gearing up to get rowdy. "I like men. She doesn't have the right parts."

Janet widened her eyes and Harper was convinced the older woman was about to say something derogatory. "Oh, well, that changes things," she said. "I didn't realize that. Then it's fine for you to live with each other."

Harper swiveled, surprised. "That doesn't bother you?"

"Honey, you can't help how you're born," Janet chided. "If you judge this boy for that, you'll be judged for something worse."

Harper couldn't help being impressed. "You take a lot of people by surprise, don't you?"

Janet shrugged. "I don't like being predictable."

"You said it, sister." Zander extended his hand to do a knuckle bump with Janet. He grinned like a crazy person when she absentmindedly mimicked the gesture. "Okay, back to business. You don't have a ghost. You have a poltergeist. We've put together a modified dreamcatcher and we're hopeful it will work, but it might not be strong enough."

"What's the difference?" Janet asked. She appeared genuinely curious.

"A ghost generally remains behind because it has unfinished business or was somehow traumatized by death," Harper explained, tugging her hair into a ponytail holder. "A poltergeist holds onto a buttload of residual anger from the soul's former life, and over time that anger manifests in dangerous situations."

Janet furrowed her brow. "So you're saying that my sister wants to kill me?"

"I'm saying that whatever is in there is angry and we need to be very careful how we approach the situation," Harper clarified. "I'm going to be honest with you … I think we would be better trying to draw the spirit outside rather than deal with it inside."

"How come?"

"Because there are a lot of things in that barn that can kill a person," Zander answered. "We like helping ghosts move on, but we draw the line at letting them kill us during the process."

"I hear that," Janet muttered, bumping her fist into Zander's and earning a gleeful smile. "So how do you want to draw her out?"

"I'm thinking that we'll put the dreamcatcher on the other side of the door and use you as bait," Harper replied. "She probably doesn't like us, but she seems to have built up a lot of animosity where you're concerned."

"That's the way of family," Janet said, shaking her head ruefully. "I'm game if you are. Where are your other workers?"

Harper and Zander exchanged a quick look.

"This could get dangerous," Zander said, choosing his words carefully. "It's not a normal situation. Harper and I own the business together so we believe we should be the ones to take the risk."

Janet studied Zander a moment, her expression thoughtful. "That sounds like a very brave thing to do."

"Thank you."

"It also sounds like horse pucky," Janet added. "You two are giddy and in love with each other after a big fight so you don't want to deal with other people if you don't have to. Don't bother denying it. It's written all over your faces."

"We just told you that we're not a couple," Harper protested.

"There are different kinds of love," Janet shot back. "You two love each other. It's kind of cute but also a little annoying. It's just like how I loved my sister – even though she was often a lazy idiot who had whiny qualities that made me want to kick out her teeth – and I put off calling you folks for a long time because I didn't want to hurt her."

"What changed your mind?"

"The fact that you can't hold on forever," Janet replied, squaring her shoulders. "I'm the only one alive out of all of my siblings and I want to enjoy what's left of my time. I don't think that's too much to ask."

"It's definitely not too much to ask," Harper confirmed, flashing a smile as she gripped the hand-woven dreamcatcher in her hand. "Are you ready to do this?"

"As ready as I'll ever be."

"Then let's get in position," Harper said. "If we're lucky, this will be an easy day and then we can celebrate with ice cream. There's nothing better than ice cream."

"I THINK you might've ruined my appetite for ice cream … forever."

Zander looked horrified forty minutes later as he reached out a tentative hand to help Janet to her feet – snatching his fingers back a moment before he touched her. She was covered from head to foot in a filmy substance, white goo oozing around her shoulders and hands.

"Me, too," Harper muttered, shaking her head. "I'm so depressed."

"You're depressed?" Janet's eyes flashed with distaste. "I'm covered in … slime."

"Think of it this way," Zander offered. "Now you can say you starred in your own version of *Ghostbusters*."

Janet narrowed her eyes to dangerous brown slits. "Don't make me kick you."

"I still don't understand how this happened," Harper mused, giving Janet a wide berth as she circled the woman. "I didn't know a poltergeist could affect a human environment this way. I mean … I guess it makes sense. A poltergeist runs on anger and rage to move things … or throw things. This leftover residue would seem to suggest that poltergeists are so powerful they can manifest an energy waste product."

Harper didn't consider herself a science nerd, but she was completely fascinated with the slime the poltergeist left behind when it attacked Janet. The plan had, for the most part, worked exactly how they thought it would. The poltergeist was faster than expected, though, so Harper and Zander had to chase it down as it attacked Janet. Thankfully the modified dreamcatcher was strong enough to force the spirit to pass over. If it wasn't – if the poltergeist escaped – things would've spiraled quickly.

"I'm so glad you're having a good time with your science experiment," Janet said dryly, rolling her eyes. "You should write a book about it or something."

"I've been trying to get Harp to write a book for years, but she doesn't like the limelight," Zander offered. "I considered writing one myself – I love the limelight – but fame is a fickle beast and I don't want people to love me just for my looks."

Harper snorted. "That's your dream scenario."

"Yes, well, you could've backed me up anyway," Zander sniffed. "I prefer people thinking I'm humble."

"I'm going to put my foot in your humble behind if you don't help me up," Janet warned, extending her hand. She ignored Zander's grimace as he touched her and groaned as she finally lumbered to her feet. "I can't believe that just happened." Now that she was upright, she seemed amazed by the turn of events.

"It was definitely interesting," Harper said, checking the laptop computer screen she removed from the office earlier in the day. "There's plenty of data here for Eric to go through. That should make him happy."

"Oh, don't kid yourself," Zander admonished. "He's going to be totally ticked off because we cut him out of the takedown. Molly is going to organize a mutiny because she thought she was going to be primary."

"We both know that wouldn't have been safe."

"I believe that's what I told you the first day we came out here."

"Yes, but I was mad at you that day so I couldn't agree with you without looking like an idiot. I'm so glad we made up." Harper beamed as she wiggled her nose and caused Zander to chuckle.

"Me, too." Zander exhaled heavily before rolling his neck until it cracked. "At least we have the data … and everyone survived."

"And I have a safe barn," Janet added. "Follow me to the house. I'll write you a check. You might have to wait a minute until I wash off some of this … gunk … but I would say that was money well earned."

"You did most of the work," Harper pointed out.

"Yes, but you had the know-how," Janet said. "Don't sell yourself short. That was kind of an amazing thing we all did today."

Zander beamed. "I couldn't have said it better myself."

THIRTY MINUTES later Janet was scrubbed and clean and dressed in a fresh set of overalls as she joined Zander and Harper in the kitchen. Despite her age, she seemed none the worse for wear. That's when something occurred to Harper.

"Janet, how well did you know Arthur Fleming?"

Janet's face was pinched with surprise when she swiveled. "Arthur? Why are you asking about Arthur?"

"Because we just unearthed a dead body in his backyard and I'm mildly curious if you knew him," Harper replied, sipping her glass of iced tea. "Most people tend to think he was disagreeable and mean, but not everyone could've hated him. I'm not sure that's possible."

"Nobody is hated by everybody," Janet said sagely. "Arthur was pretty darned close, though. I hadn't heard about the body. I don't even watch regular television now. With Netflix – and all those lesbians doing wacky things in prison – there's no need."

Harper pressed her lips together to keep from laughing. It was a serious conversation, after all. Er, well, kind of. "Her name was Tess Hilliard. Does that name ring a bell to you?"

"Of course," Janet answered, not missing a beat. "Tess Hilliard was the woman Arthur knocked up. They were having an affair."

Harper widened her eyes, surprised. "You knew about that? I thought you didn't like Arthur."

"I couldn't stand Arthur. He was a real jackass. I did like Annette on occasion … usually only when she had a few drinks in her, though."

"Wait … did Annette tell you about Tess and the baby?" Zander asked, leaning forward.

Janet nodded. "It was a big scandal there for about six months," she explained. "Whisper Cove was even smaller back then – if you can imagine that – and we had weekly social gatherings at town hall. It was a potluck and everyone brought a dish.

"Arthur never came, mind you, but Annette always put in an appearance," she continued. "You weren't technically supposed to drink at those things, but that didn't stop anyone. We all shared flasks and gossiped once the eating was done and one night after drinking way more than she should've done, Annette told us about Arthur and Tess."

"What did she say?"

"She said that Arthur wasn't even trying to hide what he was doing and that she thought he was purposely flaunting the relationship in front of her to be mean," Janet answered. "You have to understand that Annette and Arthur never liked one another. The longer they stayed married, the deeper the animosity grew. They got off on upsetting one another. I think they had sex exactly three times – and that's how they got the children – and slept in separate bedrooms after that."

"Do you think that Arthur was going to leave Annette for Tess?"

"No way." Janet vehemently shook her head. "Annette had Arthur by the balls and everyone knew it. That house was in her family's name so if Arthur took off with Tess he would've had no claim to the house and had to pay spousal support to Annette at the same time."

"It sounds as if he was stuck," Zander mused, rubbing the back of his neck. "Did Tess pressure Arthur anyway?"

"Oh, yeah. That was common knowledge. She popped out that kid and Arthur was in a real mess. He didn't really want another kid and even though he liked Tess he didn't want to spend the rest of his life with her."

"Well, there's your motive," Harper said. "Tess was going after Arthur to leave Annette without realizing that he couldn't leave Annette without going broke."

"It was a vicious circle," Zander said.

"It all makes sense, though," Harper said. "The only thing that doesn't match up is the fact that Annette must've recognized Tess in those photos she found. Why bring them in if she recognized the woman?"

"Maybe she didn't realize she recognized her," Zander suggested. "You said she's suffering from dementia. Maybe she forgot."

"I guess that's a possibility." Harper downed the rest of her iced tea and then got to her feet. "There's only one way to find out, though. We need to ask Annette exactly what she remembers about that time period."

"Good luck with that," Janet said. "That's one secret Annette would happily leave dead and buried."

"Which makes me wonder why she dug it up in the first place," Harper said. "Thank you so much for the information, Janet. We'll show ourselves out."

Seventeen

"There's my girl. What's going on?"

Jared smiled as he glanced up from the file on his desk, his eyes lighting up as Zander and Harper strode into the police department shortly before lunch.

"I'm fine," Zander replied dryly. "That's a very insensitive thing to say, though. I'm not a girl even though I'm totally pretty as a picture. It's nice to be wanted, though."

Jared's smile tipped down. "I'm glad to see you're feeling like your old self again," he intoned. "That won't make me feel bad in the slightest when I put a new lock on Harper's bedroom door so we can keep you out unless expressly invited in."

Zander made an exaggerated face as he clutched at his heart. "You wound me. Do you really think that's going to change anything?"

"Yup."

"Let me rephrase that," Zander suggested. "Do you really think I'll let that change anything?"

Jared narrowed his eyes to dangerous slits as Mel made a big show of clearing his throat and stepping between the two men.

"Hello, nephew. If you're here to cause trouble, perhaps you should turn around and take your attitude elsewhere."

Zander maintained eye contact with Jared for a few moments, a silent challenge passing between them, and then he squared his shoulders and focused on his uncle.

"You were my favorite relative until that. Now I don't like you at all. I can't believe you're taking his side over mine."

"And I can't believe you're picking a fight with an armed man," Mel shot back. "I'm still your favorite relative. We both know it."

"Only because there's so little to choose from."

"I'm fine with that," Mel said, perching on the edge of Jared's desk as he looked over Harper and Zander. They looked happy and excited. That was a big upgrade from what Jared described the day before. "I'm guessing you two are infatuated with one another again. Who apologized first this time?"

"We apologized at the exact same time," Harper replied.

"That's not what happened," Zander said, rolling his eyes. "She apologized to me and I graciously accepted. Then I opened my arms and pulled her in for a hug, thus wiping away the days of unhappiness and self-doubt as they weighed down her weary soul."

"You watch way too much *Dr. Phil*," Jared chided, shaking his head. "She hasn't been unhappy. She's been with me. That's a reason to be happy, just for the record."

"It definitely is," Harper agreed, beaming as she shuffled closer to Jared and kissed his cheek. "The mere sight of you thrills me to the very core of my being."

"Oh, you're both being all weird with the words today," Jared teased, although he happily accepted the kiss and grabbed her hand before she could wander off. "I'll take it. While you haven't been unhappy the past few days, you have been in a bit of a funk. I'm glad you two made up."

"Me, too," Zander said. "I was ready to cry in my half-fat mocha latte this morning. It was a terrible feeling."

"Yes, well, I'm still agitated with you," Jared commented. "We need to have a discussion about your early morning activities. Do you want to do that now or wait until we don't have an audience?"

"I don't care when we do it," Zander replied, blasé. "I'm not going to change my habits. We both know it. I can pretend to promise to stay out of Harper's bed and you can pretend to believe me, but we both know it's not going to happen over the long haul."

Jared pursed his lips, rolling his neck to stave off the annoyance. "How about we compromise?"

Zander cocked his head, suspicious. "What did you have in mind? Wait … before you answer that, let me be upfront, I'm not going to take it well if you try banning me from Harper's room. I'm never going to be able to agree to a compromise that involves shunning."

"Good grief. You're so dramatic," Mel intoned. "How can you not understand that the man doesn't appreciate you climbing into bed with him and his woman when they're naked? It seems to me that would be common sense."

"Did you just call me 'his woman,' Mel?" Harper's eyes flashed.

"You know what I mean."

"I'm not sure I do."

Mel looked to Jared for help. "Do you want to step in here? I'm standing up for you, after all."

"And you're doing a marvelous job," Jared teased. "I know better than referring to a woman as property, though. As for the compromise, I want to pick a specific day of the week when you can hop into bed with us. That way we'll know to get dressed the night before."

"One day?" Zander knew he sounded unbelievably whiny, but he couldn't muster the energy to care. "That's not enough."

"One day." Jared was firm. "You guys work together and live together. I think one day is more than fair."

Zander glanced at Harper. "Are you okay with this?"

Harper looked caught as she glanced between them, Jared's words from the previous evening echoing throughout her mind. "I *am* okay with it," she said after a beat, internally smiling when she saw Jared jolt. He obviously thought she was going to take Zander's side. "We need to set some boundaries. Now that Shawn is going to be visiting more often, I think the boundaries are as good for you as they are for me."

"But ... ."

"Think about it, Zander," Harper prodded. "Shawn isn't going to like it if you leave him in your bed and hop into mine. We need to come up with a schedule that benefits everyone."

"So you're picking Jared over me?" Zander was bordering on mutinous.

Harper answered without hesitation. "In this instance, yes."

"Oh, whatever." Zander threw his hands up in the air and made a disgusted sound in the back of his throat. "Fine. We'll do one day a week. Does that make you happy, Jared?"

"For now," Jared replied, his chest warming with pleasure. He hadn't expected Harper to put her foot down so quickly. "I'll be even happier when you guys tell me what you're doing here. I thought you had a job today."

"We did," Harper said, returning to reality. "We were out at the Markowitz farm. We got rid of the poltergeist."

"That's good, right?"

Harper nodded. "While we were talking to Janet, though, she let something slip about the Tess Hilliard case."

Jared leaned forward, intrigued. "Oh, yeah? What's that?"

"She said Annette knew about Tess and the baby," Harper replied. "She said Annette let it slip at a potluck meal one night. She had too much to drink and it all spilled out."

"Huh." Jared rubbed his chin as he extended his legs under his desk. "I guess that changes things a bit, huh? If Annette knew, she becomes a strong suspect."

"Annette always hated Arthur, though," Mel pointed out. "Why would she care?"

"Because it's one thing to hate your husband," Harper answered. "It's quite another to let him find happiness with another woman. Janet also said that Annette wasn't happy about the admission and she considered it a betrayal."

"I would think that would be a given," Jared said, his eyes shifting between Harper and Mel. "I guess that means we have to go back to the Fleming house."

"I already questioned her yesterday," Mel said. "She didn't remember."

"Matthew also said his mother was dealing with dementia and remembered different things depending on the day," Jared said. "I don't see where we have much choice. We have to exert due diligence here. We have to at least try."

Mel didn't look thrilled with the suggestion. "Okay, but I'm going to let you handle it this time. I think she likes you better than me."

"Oh, how can that even be possible?" Zander deadpanned. "You're so sweet and nice and ... oh, wait, I must've been thinking of someone else who didn't turn on his favorite nephew."

Mel flicked Zander's ear and shook his head. "You're a pain in the keister."

"You love me anyway."

Jared's eyes were somber as they shifted to Harper. "Do you want to go with me?"

Harper immediately nodded. "I want to see if Tess's ghost is back out there. This will give me a reason to wander around while you're questioning Annette."

"Okay." Jared extended his hand as he stood. "I'll buy you lunch as a reward once we're finished."

"That's good," Harper said. "I'm buying you dinner tonight so it will even out."

"You're buying me dinner?" Jared looked pleased and surprised.

Harper nodded. "I am. We're going on a double date with Zander and Shawn."

"Oh, that sounds like a good idea."

"We're doing it at Jason's restaurant so we can dance after dinner."

Jared groaned, his lips twisting. "Great. Now I'm going to fight him off, too."

Zander sympathetically patted Jared's back. "He's got nothing on you, pal. I've seen both of you without your clothes on – granted, Jason was a long time ago, but I have a good memory – and you're much better to look at it in the buff. You've got this sewn up for the long haul."

Jared fought the urge to grab Zander's head and hold it in his armpit while he rubbed his knuckles over the man's always-perfect hairline. "You make me tired."

Zander was unruffled. "You'll live."

"YOU'RE BACK."

Matthew's face reflected surprise when he opened the door twenty minutes later. He was dressed down in simple jeans and a T-shirt, his face grimy from what looked to be steady work as he packed up the house. Even though he flashed a smile, Harper knew he wasn't in a welcoming mood.

"We are," Jared agreed, bobbing his head. "I need to talk to your mother."

"She's sleeping."

Jared glanced at Harper, unsure. It wasn't that he didn't believe Annette was sleeping – although it was a distinct possibility that Matthew was merely being overprotective and covering for her. It was more that Matthew's attitude chafed given the circumstances.

"We don't have a lot of choice in the matter," Jared said, his tone even. "We found out that your mother knew about the Tess Hilliard affair … and the baby."

Matthew stilled, his body unnaturally stiff. "I'm sorry but … what baby?"

"Tess had a baby before she died," Jared replied. "We just found out about him yesterday. I'm sorry to drop it on you like that – with no warning – but it came as a surprise to us, too."

"You can't be serious." Matthew placed his hands on his hips and stared down the hallway that led to

Annette's parlor. Harper had a sneaking suspicion that the woman was watching her stories rather than napping. "I don't want to be crude, but are you sure the child belonged to my father? I mean … from everything you've said … this woman got around."

"I guess that's a fair point." Jared's heart went out to Matthew. The man looked weary and beaten down. He was in an uncomfortable situation. He had a dead father and sick mother – neither of whom he was particularly close with – and now he found out that he might have a half-brother running around. "I don't believe a DNA test was ever done. He was raised by his aunt and is fairly successful. He knows the identity of his mother, but I don't believe he intends to approach your family for anything, if that's what you're worried about."

"I have no idea what I'm worried about," Matthew admitted, briefly pressing his eyes shut. "I'm so tired and this is so much to deal with."

"I understand that and I'm sorry," Jared said. "Tess Hilliard was murdered, though, and we need to close the case … one way or another."

"Just to play devil's advocate, I thought you couldn't determine a cause of death. How do you know it wasn't an accident?"

The question took Jared by surprise. "Someone still buried her. Someone still took photos of her dead body. There's blood in the photographs. That seems to indicate foul play rather than an accident to me."

"I guess that's a reasonable assumption," Matthew muttered, shaking his head. "What will happen to my mother if you believe she killed Tess?"

Things clicked into place for Jared. Matthew wasn't being standoffish because he wanted to blame the victim –

which was his initial assessment. No, Matthew was worried about his mother.

"I'm not sure," Jared answered, opting for honesty. "It's an odd case. Given her age and other issues, though, I can pretty much guarantee she won't end up in prison. She might, however, have to relocate to a hospital."

"Would I have any input on that? I mean … I want her to get the very best treatment available. She doesn't remember any of this. I can guarantee that."

Harper wasn't so sure – Annette did go out of her way to deliver the photographs to the police department, after all – but she wisely kept her opinion to herself.

"It might be better that she doesn't remember," Jared said. "She might've stumbled across the photos and been confused … or perhaps her subconscious got the better of her. We may never know. I still have to ask her a few questions, though."

Matthew looked torn, but finally he heaved out a sigh and nodded his head. "Please don't pressure her too much if she doesn't remember. She gets flustered if you ask a question more than twice … and then she gets ornery and angry if you hound her."

"I don't want to make things worse," Jared said. "I just want to find out the truth."

"Okay then. This way."

Matthew led Harper and Jared toward the parlor, the blonde dragging her feet as she followed. She was lost in thought, a myriad of possibilities floating through her head. Jared and Matthew entered the parlor ahead of her as Harper lingered in the hallway. As she lifted her sky blue eyes, Harper locked gazes with a ghostly Tess as she floated by the kitchen door.

Harper opened her mouth, a question on her lips. Tess merely shook her head, her eyes dark and sad. Harper remembered where she was – and whom she was with – before anything slipped out of her mouth. That didn't stop her from staring at the ghost, who looked sad and forlorn.

Finally, Tess was the one who broke eye contact first … and faded away to that place ghosts rest between visits … wherever that was.

Was this the end? Harper had trouble wrapping her mind around the outcome. Punishing Annette now seemed cruel and unusual. Letting Tess's murder go unchecked was hardly a tolerable solution, though. In the end, no one was going to be happy.

Harper rested her head against the wall and listened to Jared talk to Annette, his tone soothing as the woman answered a series of questions. It didn't sound as if today was a good day for walking down memory lane.

For once, there was no clear-cut answer. There was no right or wrong. Harper found that to be the most troubling aspect. Who do you blame when there's no one to punish?

EIGHTEEN

"I'm sorry I'm late. I got held up at the gym."

Shawn, his khakis pressed to perfection and his shirt highlighting his eyes, exchanged a quick kiss with Zander as he sat in the open deck chair. His hair was windblown – since Jason's restaurant was located on the lake that happened a lot – but he still managed to look as if he'd stepped off the pages of a magazine. Harper couldn't help but be impressed.

"That's okay," Jared said, leaning back and resting his arm on the back of Harper's chair. "We've only been here five minutes."

"That's good." Shawn looked relieved as he smiled at everyone in turn. "One of the treadmills broke down and I had to fix it before I left."

"I heard someone new bought the gym about four months ago, but then I forgot all about it," Harper admitted, sipping a glass of wine. "How long have you been in town?"

"I technically live in Clinton Township," Shawn explained. "I still have five months on my lease, but then I'm looking for a place closer to here. The commute is only twenty minutes right now, so it's not terrible, but I would like to completely eradicate it in a few months. I've always loved Whisper Cove and have been saving up to buy my own gym for quite some time. When this opportunity arose and the price was right … I guess I kind of felt it was destiny."

Harper smiled; delighted by the shy look Shawn and Zander exchanged. Zander had gone on so many dates she'd lost count, but she couldn't ever remember him bringing someone home. He generally just explained what was wrong with the guy in question and moved on relatively quickly. He was clearly smitten with Shawn, though.

"How did you guys meet?" Jared asked, rubbing his thumb over Harper's bare shoulder. She'd opted to dress up for the evening, wearing a flowered slip dress and heeled sandals. She fancied herself a jeans and T-shirt type of girl, but she enjoyed dressing up on occasion.

"We met at the gym," Zander supplied.

"I know that," Jared said dryly. "You live in the gym. Did you have some cute little flirtation going before someone invited someone else to coffee or something, though? Did you compare muscles before kissing?"

"Oh, that." Shawn's cheeks colored, making him even more handsome than moments before, if that was even possible. "I'd noticed him coming in for almost two weeks after I took ownership – that was a little more than three months ago, mind you – but I was too nervous to ask him out. I wasn't even sure he was gay at first."

Jared and Harper exchanged a quick look. Zander wasn't known for hiding his sexuality.

"That doesn't sound like Zander," Harper pointed out.

"Well, I asked around about him," Shawn clarified. "I thought he was really cute and he was always friendly. He often seemed distracted, though, and he ran out on secret missions all of the time."

Jared cocked an eyebrow. "Secret missions?"

"Well, I thought they were secret missions," Shawn conceded. "One day I saw him with Harper in town and they were laughing and having a good time. Up until then I was pretty sure he was gay. When I saw him with Harper I was … um … confused.

"I decided to watch him a little bit instead of making a move because I didn't want to be embarrassed and find out he was straight," he continued. "Whisper Cove is a small town and I didn't want to risk offending anyone. I figured out pretty quickly that everyone here has known everyone else for the bulk of his or her lives so they're up in everyone else's business."

"Isn't that the truth," Jared muttered, shaking his head.

"So I kind of hung around town hoping to see him," Shawn said. "I didn't want him to only think of me when he was going to the gym – I guess that sounds lame – so I started taking walks every afternoon. I figured out pretty quickly that he and Harper went on ice cream runs almost daily in the afternoon."

"Yes, my Heart loves her ice cream." Jared affectionately brushed a strand of her hair away from her face. "Sometimes she can't stop herself from eating gallons of it and she ends up puking, but that doesn't stop her. She's like a machine."

"Ha, ha," Harper intoned, wrinkling her nose. "Go on with your story."

"That's just it," Shawn said, smirking. "I saw Jared and you together on one of my walks and couldn't figure out what was going on. You and Zander were always so tactile with one another – you held hands and tickled each other and stuff – and I had pretty much resigned myself to the fact that you were together.

"Then I saw you and Jared and you were holding hands," he continued. "There was a different edge to your relationship. That much was obvious.

"At first I told myself that you and Zander broke up or something, but then I found out you lived together and realized that was unlikely," he said. "Then I wondered if you were cheating on Zander and I got a little offended on his behalf."

Harper couldn't help but giggle. She was having a good time. "I don't think publicly dating two men in a town the size of Whisper Cove would be very smart. You'd never be able to keep that a secret."

"I know that now," Shawn conceded. "Then one night, a few weeks ago, I saw you and Jared walking on the beach together. I always thought you and Zander looked at each other with a lot of love, but the way you looked at Jared made me realize that you loved them both – only in different ways."

Harper pursed her lips and worked overtime to refrain from shifting in her seat. She'd never admitted her love to Jared. Er, well, not yet at least. She thought it was too soon. He hadn't either, which was okay with her because she figured they had plenty of time. She didn't want him to feel pressured by Shawn's simple statement.

"Basically you realized she was only having sex with one of us," Jared teased, amused. If he was bothered by Shawn's love observation, he didn't show it. "And since I'm better looking and altogether more dashing, you knew right away it was me."

"You suck," Zander muttered, although his lips twitched as he shook his head.

Shawn barked out a laugh. "I just knew you guys were together romantically," he clarified. "Then I realized that Harper and Zander – despite how touchy-feely they are – never showed signs of romance."

"If I could be with a woman, though, it would be her," Zander cooed, causing Harper to snicker.

"Yes, well, then we'd have even bigger issues than we have now," Jared said. "I think the best man won in this instance."

"I think we both won," Zander corrected.

"I think we all won," Harper snapped, scorching Jared and Zander with a warning look. "Don't even think about picking a fake fight tonight. I'll make you two share a bed while Shawn and I get to know each other if you're not careful." Harper waited a beat to make sure Zander and Jared were done messing around. "Go on with your story, Shawn."

"There's not much left to tell," Shaw said. "The next day Zander came into the gym and I spotted him on the weight bench. I asked him to coffee and that was it."

"And how long ago was that?"

"About three weeks."

Harper wrinkled her nose. "Three weeks? You made it sound as if you'd just hooked up, Zander. I thought it was a couple of days at most." Her tone was accusatory, causing Jared and Zander to straighten in their chairs.

"Harp, it's not as bad as it sounds," Zander said hurriedly. "Don't get worked up."

"No one is getting worked up," Jared said, applying pressure to the back of Harper's neck to get her to look in his direction. "Heart, we had a long talk about this last night. You cannot run Zander's life. He made a mistake keeping information from you – and inadvertently hurting you – but it's over now."

"But … three weeks!"

Jared pressed the heel of his hand to his forehead as Harper crossed her arms over her chest. Of course that was the moment Jason arrived with a platter of appetizers. "I put together your favorites and it's on the house."

"Thank you." Shawn was understandably nervous so he focused on Jason. "This is a lovely restaurant you have here."

"Thank you." Jason's smile was genuine, but his eyes were eager as they bounced between faces. "What's going on here? I thought Harper and Zander made up."

"They did, but then I ruined it." Shawn looked miserable. "I'm so sorry, Zander. I didn't mean to start another fight."

"Don't worry about it," Zander said, his eyes never leaving Harper's face. "It's not your fault. I should've told her sooner. I was just … a nervous wreck."

Even though she was angry, Harper's heart went out to her best friend. "Why were you nervous? You've dated plenty of guys. You've dated more guys than me."

"Oh, please," Zander made a hilarious face. "You've dated like five guys. You dated this dillweed." He jerked his thumb in Jason's direction. "I told you he was a thunder stealer extraordinaire, but you didn't care. Then you dated that idiot with the floppy hair in college. He wheezed when he was having sex. I thought he was going to die of a heart attack or something when you guys were doing it."

Jared scowled. "Hey! That's an overshare."

Zander ignored him. "Then you dated that frat idiot who tried to roofie your drink."

"Wait, someone tried to roofie your drink?" Jared was appalled. "Was he arrested?"

"He didn't try to roofie my drink," Harper replied. "He accidentally spit his gum in my drink and he was trying to get it out, but Zander tackled him before he could.

It was just regular keg beer, but Zander saw a *Dateline* special the night before and was convinced that someone was trying to steal me to sell to an overseas sultan."

"Oh." Jared bit the inside of his cheek to keep from laughing. "I guess that's better."

"I don't see how," Shawn deadpanned.

"I'm clearly the cream of this crop," Jason added.

"Don't push me," Jared warned, extending a finger.

"Then there was Quinn, who we won't talk about tonight, and Jared," Zander said. "That's five guys. I've had that many dates in a week."

Harper rolled her eyes. "I'm not sure I would be bragging about that in front of your new boyfriend."

"I'm not bragging. I just like numbers. That's why I balance the books at GHI."

"And I'm clearly the cream of the entire crop," Jared said, shooting Jason a challenging look.

"I think you're more like creamed corn," Jason said, not missing a beat.

"I love creamed corn," Harper and Zander said in unison, giggling to signify the crisis had passed.

"Do you remember our lazy winter Saturdays, Harp?" Zander asked, his expression wistful. "We used to make Mrs. Grass soup and creamed corn and then sit in front of the fireplace watching horror movies."

"You guys have been friends for a long time," Shawn said. "Is there ever a time when you weren't friends? I mean … I know you guys were fighting for a few days this week … but was there ever a time you thought the friendship wouldn't survive?"

"Not even remotely," Harper said, leaning back so she could snuggle closer to Jared. "I always knew that no matter what Zander would be there. He's the best friend I've ever had … and that's never going to change."

"Right back at you, Harp." Zander's smile was so wide it split his face. "You're the best friend I've ever had, too."

"I'm still cream of the crop," Jared teased.

"Definitely." Harper kissed his cheek. "You're the cream of the corn crop."

"That sounds a little odd."

"I don't care."

"Me either." Jared planted a soft kiss on the corner of her mouth.

"Ugh, I'm going to throw up," Jason muttered, shaking his head. "Do you guys know what you want?"

"I want crab legs and lobster bisque," Harper answered immediately.

"You didn't even look at the menu," Jared pointed out.

"I've been dreaming of crab legs all day."

"I guess it's good to know that I can bribe you with seafood," Jared said. "I'll have the same thing she's having."

"Make that four orders," Zander interjected after a brief conversation with Shawn.

"That sounds good to me," Jason said. "I'll put your order in while you enjoy the appetizers. Make sure someone tells another story about Harper and me dating in high school while I'm gone, though. I love seeing how agitated Jared gets."

Jared glared at Jason's back as he stalked away, only returning to the conversation when Shawn forced the issue.

"How did you two meet?" Shawn asked, genuinely curious. "You seem very tight … and I'm not just saying that because I inadvertently stalked you because I thought you might be cheating on my future boyfriend."

Harper giggled, delighted. "It's kind of a long story."

"Not that long," Jared countered. "I moved to Whisper Cove and took a job on the force. Right away we had a body wash up on shore. I kept running into Harper in odd places – including breaking into a dead woman's house – and she told me she could see and talk to ghosts. Then I arrested her and here we are."

Harper's mouth dropped open. "That is not what happened."

"It kind of is," Zander hedged.

"There's more to the story than that," Harper said, her lower lip jutting out. "What about the part where you were attracted to me and couldn't stay away? What about the part where you let me go even though you caught me breaking the law? What about the part where you saved me from a murderous college student and kissed me?"

Jared grinned at her feigned outrage. "I could never forget one moment of that. It's ingrained in my memory forever."

Harper wanted to be angry, but his earnest expression was too adorable to be ignored. "I guess that's okay," she said, heaving out a dramatic sigh. "My feelings are still a little hurt, though."

"If I give you a massage later, will that make you feel better?"

"Yes."

"That's what I thought." Jared kissed the tip of her nose. "I promise to never to leave out that part of the story again."

"Good."

"Oh, I so want to puke," Jason intoned as he maneuvered around the table and headed for another on the far end of the deck. He carried a tray laden with goodies. "You two are so sickeningly sweet it gives me hives."

"It's probably because you're allergic to cream," Jared called to his back. "I am the cream of the crop, after all."

Harper snickered. "We really need to stop talking about cream."

"I agree," Zander said. "Let's talk about something more interesting. I know, let's talk about me. I'm always entertaining."

Harper gripped Jared's hand under the table and smiled. "No one could possibly argue with that."

NINETEEN

"You were very good tonight."

Jared shifted his hips so Harper could get more comfortable on the chaise lounger, slipping his arm around her shoulders as she made a sighing noise as she snuggled close. They opted to relax on the back porch in order to give Zander and Shawn some alone time, and Jared was thrilled with the bright evening sky – and his partner in crime. He loved the way her body felt against his, how they fit together. He never knew true peace until he found her, a sobering thought that somehow managed to be relaxing as well as enlightening.

"I was good?" Harper missed the obvious signs regarding Jared's deep thoughts and cocked a challenging eyebrow. "What is that supposed to mean?"

"Only that I was legitimately worried you would say something snotty to Shawn." Jared saw no reason to lie. "You're a wonderful and charming woman, but you and Zander have a certain rapport that takes some getting used to."

"So … you thought I would be mean to Shawn?" Harper's expression was unreadable.

"Not on purpose. I don't think you do anything out of malice."

"I once glued Zander's zipper so it wouldn't stay closed and he walked around entire the day with his fly open. That was totally out of malice because he told me I looked like a Barbie doll and I, therefore, had to sit and let him put makeup on me. It was the longest six hours of my life."

Jared's lips swished. "Very cute. That's not what I was talking about, though. I worried that you weren't quite over Zander keeping a secret from you and somehow you might accidentally explode all over Shawn. You didn't do that, though."

"I like him."

"I like him, too," Jared said. "More importantly, I think Zander likes him. That's why he didn't tell you. You know that, right?"

Harper pressed her lips together as she nodded. "He didn't know what he was feeling. We always had the same routine where his love life was concerned and when he realized this time was different he temporarily got lost. I understand why he did it."

"And you forgive him?"

"I forgive him."

"Do you still feel a little bad because you think you did something wrong and made it so it was impossible for Zander to confide in you?"

Harper's eyes widened. "How did you know that?"

"Because I know you," Jared replied, his tone teasing. "Heart, Zander loves you beyond reason. He sometimes loves you more than I'm comfortable with. This is new ground for him. I'm going to guess that he didn't have a lot of dating options growing up in Whisper Cove.

"I think he uses sarcasm as a defense mechanism and it was easier for him to date a guy for one night and then blow him off right away rather than deal with feelings he knew he'd never have," he continued. "Everything changed when he met Shawn because he really likes him."

Harper studied Jared a moment, using her index finger to trace his strong jaw line. "You have a giving heart and a keen eye. You see things others miss. You see things about Zander I miss."

"I think you were too close to the situation. You see a lot more than I do. You're magical, Heart. You can't help yourself from seeing everything. Sometimes I think that haunts you … in more ways than one."

"Like the fact that I've seen Tess twice and she refuses to talk to me?"

"Exactly like that," Jared confirmed, stroking the back of her head. "In your head you're blaming yourself."

"I'm not blaming myself."

Jared patiently waited.

"Fine. I'm not blaming myself completely." Harper heaved out a weary sigh. "Do you know what I was thinking while you were questioning Annette earlier? I kept wondering how you get justice for someone when there's no one to punish. I mean … even if you arrest Annette for killing Tess that's not justice."

"Annette will never be cleared to stand trial. She's too weak. Even if they file charges she'll simply get transferred to a hospital for observation."

"And die there."

"And die there." Jared brushed his lips against Harper's forehead. "I don't know what the answer is. Either Arthur killed her and escaped punishment or Annette did and she's about to be a prisoner in her own mind."

"And the only thing we're definitely sure about is that Tess won't get justice," Harper mused. "That doesn't seem fair, does it?"

"Life isn't fair, Heart. All we can do is our best."

"But we have no way of knowing which one of them killed Tess."

"No, but at least we found her and she's getting a chance to move on," Jared said. "Maybe that's why all of this happened. Maybe it wasn't about finding out what happened to her. Maybe it was about helping her."

"She's been here this entire time," Harper pointed out. "I've never seen her. Do you think she's been walking around that property for twenty-five years?"

"I have no idea. I hope not."

"I don't see any other alternative," Harper said. "She died twenty-five years ago and I've never seen her. I think that means she was alone there the entire time."

"What are you going to do about it?"

Harper shrugged. "I'll probably go out there tomorrow and sit by the river. Maybe she'll come to me. Maybe I'll be able to figure out a way to help her move on without making it a traumatic experience."

"I wish I could go with you, but I need to get all of the case notes together tomorrow. Mel and I both have to sign off on it before we can put it to bed. Then I need to make a few calls. If you want to wait a day … ."

"I don't want to wait. It's not as if I'm in danger out there or anything. Annette isn't going to traipse through the woods to get me or anything. I'll be okay."

"I still wish I could go with you."

The duo lapsed into comfortable silence for a moment and then Harper rolled so she was on top of him and staring into his smoldering eyes. "You promised me a massage."

The corners of Jared's mouth tipped up. "I was hoping to do it naked."

"Shawn and Zander are still in the living room. How about we compromise?"

"What did you have in mind?"

"You start rubbing me here and then finish in the bedroom."

Jared barked out a laugh as he moved his hands to her shoulders. "You drive a hard bargain."

"THEY'RE ridiculously cute."

Shawn rested his hip against the counter as he watched Jared and Harper cuddle on the back porch. They appeared to be in their own little world as they easily chatted. Shawn had no idea what they were talking about, but they were intent on each other and clearly comfortable in their emotional proximity.

"I didn't know what to think about him when he first showed up," Zander admitted. "I was all for them going out on a date, of course. Harper went a long time coasting through life after Quinn. A date was the one thing I wanted for her more than anything else."

"He's the boyfriend who died, right? You mentioned him at dinner but moved on pretty quickly."

"It would've been easier for her if he simply died. He disappeared, though. She couldn't get thoughts of him suffering out of her head. She kept imagining him crawling through the underbrush and desperately searching for help.

"Even though Mel told her that Quinn lost too much blood to survive, she couldn't deal with the not knowing," he continued. "After a few days she had no choice but to give up hope that he was alive even though I think she was still coming up with elaborate survival scenarios in the back of her mind. She mentioned amnesia once or twice. That's when I banned her from watching *General Hospital*."

Shawn flashed a sympathetic smile. "That must have been hard on both of you."

"I never liked him so I felt guilty. There was nothing I could do for him, though, so I focused on Harper. I was content to leave her to mourn – even when she got manic and searched the woods by herself for months – but when she refused to even look at another guy mild worry turned into outright panic."

"She spent years alone until Jared came around," Shawn mused. "That must've been a relief."

"It was at first. I thought she would go out on a date or two with him, get horizontal because it was obvious that was going to happen given their chemistry, and then they would go their separate ways."

Shawn couldn't help but be surprised. "You didn't think they would make it? They're so … in tune … with one another, though."

"I didn't think they would make it. Then, when I realized they were going to make it – because they're going to make it all the way – I got worried for a different reason."

Shawn understood what Zander was trying to say before he even uttered the words. "You thought he was going to take her away from you."

"I *knew* he was going to take her away from me. They belong together. Part of me was jealous, though. I didn't want to lose her."

"He's not taking her away from you, though," Shawn pointed out. "He's merely adding another corner to the arrangement. You guys couldn't be a straight line to one another forever. He simply made you a triangle."

"And now we're a square," Zander said, his lips twitching. "Aren't you going to ask why I didn't tell her about you? I know you must be curious."

Shawn shrugged. "I already know."

"You do?"

"You liked me so much you didn't know what to do with the feelings. You didn't tell her right away because you convinced yourself it wouldn't go anywhere. Then, the longer you waited, the harder it got to tell the truth. It spiraled and you melted under the pressure."

"Oh, you really do know me."

Shawn chuckled. "I'm getting there."

"SO WHAT do you think will happen when you put your file together?" Harper asked, her mind clouding at the edges as Jared's fingers worked their magic.

"I don't know. I'll type everything up and sit down with the county prosecutor. There really is no way of knowing what happened unless Annette's memory clears and she decides to admit to a murder – which I find unlikely."

"Then what happens?"

"Then we close the file."

"Do you think you'll be able to let it go? I'm not sure I could. I always want to know all of the answers."

"I know you do," Jared teased, shifting lower on the lounger and tugging her up at the same time so they were virtually mouth-to-mouth. "That's one of the things I like most about you."

"Oh, yeah? What are the others?"

"Are you fishing for compliments?"

"Maybe."

"Well, I guess you've had a tough week so you deserve a few," Jared said, his eyes lit with mirth. "I like that you're loyal … and cute … and cuddly … and you look flat out adorable when you put on mud masks with Zander."

"You could do that, too. It would do wonders for your pores."

Jared ignored the feigned dig. "I like that you're smart ... and sarcastic ... and incredibly sexy."

"Oh, really?" Harper arched an eyebrow as she slipped her hand under his shirt. She felt his pulse ratchet up a notch as her fingers brushed over his chest. "How sexy?"

"Well, let me tell you." Jared slammed his mouth into Harper's, causing her to squeal as he gripped her hips and held her close. The need between them was fervent and sweet at the same time. They clung to each other for a few moments and then Jared shifted out from underneath Harper and grabbed her around the waist before tossing her over his shoulder.

"What are you doing?" Harper asked, breathless.

"Turning in for the night. I'm exhausted."

"Oh, and here I was hoping you were gearing yourself up to play a rousing game of 'What's Under the Covers.'"

Jared barked out a laugh as he headed toward the back door. "Something tells me we'll be able to figure it out."

Harper giggled hysterically as Jared opened the door, never lifting her head to study the taciturn ghost watching from the shadows. For her part, the spirit of Tess Hilliard could do nothing but watch ... and grieve the life she never got to fully live.

"WHAT THE ... ?"

Zander jerked up his head – removing his lips from Shawn's in the process – and glared at Jared and Harper as they tromped through the house. They were making a lot of noise … and ruining the romantic environment he'd painstakingly set up.

"We're going to bed," Jared announced.

"Well, great," Zander intoned, making a disgusted face. "Do you think you could do it without giving us a floor show?"

"Apparently not." Jared's tone was breezy. "Just for the record, I'm locking the door and we will be naked when we wake up tomorrow morning. If you climb in that bed with us … ."

"Oh, don't bother," Zander said, waving off the threat. "I have other things on my mind. I have no interest in seeing you naked."

"I do," Harper said, grinning as Jared swung her body toward the hallway. "I can't wait to see you naked."

"Wishes do come true, Heart. We're almost there."

"And now I want to puke," Zander muttered.

"I think they're adorable," Shawn said, smiling brightly. "I really like them."

"Thank you," Harper called out. "I really like you, too."

Zander remained quiet until he heard Harper's door slam shut and a lock engage on the other side. When he turned to Shawn, he was irritated. "Don't encourage them. They don't need help being schmaltzy. They exude it like musk."

"I wondered what that smell was. I thought you were burning incense or something."

TWENTY

"Good morning, gentlemen."

Jared was in a ridiculously good mood the next day as he strolled out of Harper's bedroom – the blonde at his heels – and made his way to the kitchen.

Zander stood behind the counter island, a spatula in his hand, and raised his eyebrows. "You're a sick man, Jared Monroe."

Jared balked. "What did I do now?"

"I know what you did last night," Zander said. "That's all that matters. You sick … sick … pervert. I heard the catcalling … and the giggling … and the very odd humming."

"I told you he would hear that," Jared said to Harper, his eyes lit with amusement. "You'll have to be quieter next time."

"It was a game," Harper explained, pouring a mug of coffee before sitting at the table.

"A very fun game," Jared intoned, dropping a kiss on the back of her neck and moving toward the coffee pot.

"Sick," Zander hissed.

Harper decided to change the subject. "What's for breakfast, Zander? I'm starving."

"I'm sure you are. You worked up an appetite." Zander's eyes were dangerous slits. "For hours … and hours … and hours."

"Why … are … you … talking … so … slowly … this … morning?" Jared asking, going all out as he amped up his irritation efforts.

"Because I didn't sleep well last night. There was so much noise I'm not sure how anyone could sleep. You know I'm cranky if I don't get my nine hours."

"Ignore him." Shawn was bright-eyed and enthusiastic despite the early hour. "He slept fine. We had a good laugh about the catcalling. I didn't know a chick could be so … um … ."

"Vulgar?" Zander prodded.

"I was going to say vivacious." Shawn's flashed an impish grin. "So, what is everyone doing today?"

"I have to go the office," Jared replied. "I need to write up a report detailing the two scenarios we're dealing with. Then I have to forward it to the prosecutor. Either way, I don't expect the case to move forward, but I need an official ruling so I can close it."

"So if Annette is the guilty party she'll get away with it?" Zander flipped a pancake as he knit his eyebrows together. "That doesn't sound fair, does it?"

"Not for Tess, no," Harper replied, warming her hands on the sides of the coffee mug. "Putting her in prison when she can't remember things from day to day and has no recollection of what she did or why she did it isn't fair either."

"I get that," Zander said. "Still, Tess didn't get any closure. How are you going to help her spirit move on?"

"I'm going to go out there and try to talk to her today," Harper replied.

"How are you going to explain that to Matthew?"

"I'm not going to park at the house," Harper answered. "I'm going to park by the hiking trail and walk a mile back and approach the river from that direction."

"That sounds like a lot of work," Zander said. "Why don't you just explain that you need to look around the property one last time. That way you won't have to walk in this heat. It's supposed to get humid this afternoon."

"Because I'm not a cop and I don't have a legitimate reason to be on that property," Harper explained. "It's only a mile. I'll take a bottle of water and be fine. The two times I've seen Tess's spirit she's been weak. I don't think she's really interested in staying. I think telling her she has the option to leave will be enough to free her.

"If that doesn't work, though, we'll put together an outing and use a dreamcatcher," she continued. "It shouldn't be a big deal. Tess has no reason to stay. It's too late for vengeance."

"Annette is still here," Zander pointed out. "If she's the guilty party it might make sense for Tess to hang around until she gets her comeuppance."

"Yes, but that's never going to happen," Harper said. "Matthew is taking Annette away. She'll be gone. Tess won't have her to haunt and the house will be empty until it sells. There honestly is nothing left here for Tess."

"Okay." Zander started doling out pancakes on plates. "I don't think you should go alone, though. I have a meeting with the bank about opening a money market account for our business funds. Can't you wait to do this until after two or so?"

Harper made a face. "Why don't you want me to go alone? It's not as if I'll be in danger."

"You find danger wherever you go," Zander pointed out.

"Yes, but Annette isn't a threat to me and Arthur is dead." The obstinate tilt of Harper's head was meant to send a message. "What do you think is going to happen?"

"Probably nothing," Zander conceded.

"I'm fully capable of taking care of myself," Harper reminded him, her hackles rising.

"No one said you're not, Wonder Woman," Zander shot back. "You're still my best friend and you're going to be out in the middle of the woods by yourself. I would prefer if you had backup."

"You hate the woods."

"I love you, though," Zander said. "Just … wait."

Harper rolled her eyes and sipped her coffee. "I'm not going to wait. I don't need a babysitter." She said the words so low she wasn't sure anyone heard her. The look Zander shot in her direction told her otherwise.

"Before this gets out of hand, I would like to weigh in," Jared interjected, holding up his hands when Zander's eyes flashed. "You guys just made up. Let's not turn this into another fight so soon."

"I second that," Shawn offered.

"This is between Harper and me," Zander warned. "This is our business."

"And no one is paying us for this job so it's more of a public service," Harper said.

"That doesn't make it any less dangerous," Zander argued.

Harper batted her eyes as she turned to Jared. "Tell him he's being unreasonable."

Jared made a big show of swallowing a large gulp of coffee before resting his mug on the table. The look he shot Harper made her queasy a second before he opened his mouth. "I think Zander is right and you shouldn't go alone."

"Ha!" Zander hopped from one foot to the other. He was surprised and grateful for the help, but he also felt vindicated.

"We talked about this last night," Harper complained. "You said you were fine with it."

"No, I kept my opinion to myself because I didn't want to ruin our night," Jared corrected. "I was going to voice my concerns this morning … and then run out and hide at the office like a little girl when you had your inevitable meltdown."

Shawn snorted, amused. He enjoyed watching the threesome play with one another, even if one part of the triangle was being overly petulant.

"Jared, I'm going to be fine. What could possibly happen?"

"Well, for starters, you could get surprised by a ghost and accidentally fall in the river and drown."

Harper's mouth dropped open. "It's like three feet deep. I can swim."

"Not if you hit your head and you're unconscious."

Harper refused to back down. "What are the odds of that happening?"

"What are the odds of a ghost bringing us together? What are the odds of a dentist going after you and Zander under a table? What are the odds of a ghost finding us at a family hotel and revealing an old secret that just happened to coincide with a new murder? Don't talk to me about the odds."

Harper's expression was mutinous as she locked gazes with Jared. "I'm not a child."

"No, but you're very important to me," Jared said, his voice softening. "Can't you wait until this afternoon?"

Harper knew that was an option, but she didn't like people telling her what to do. "No."

"How did I know you were going to say that?" Jared tapped his foot as he pinched the bridge of his nose and stared at the ceiling.

"I guess I can rearrange the bank meeting," Zander muttered.

"Actually, I have a better idea," Shawn offered. "My assistant Sylvia is running the gym today and I have nothing going on. How about I go out to the property with Harper? I have no idea what to do around a ghost, but I love to hike and it would give me a chance to see what you guys do."

Jared pursed his lips as he considered the option. "There you go, Heart. It's a solution we all can live with. You won't be alone and you'll be able to grill Shawn about his relationship with Zander on your way out to the river."

Harper wanted to argue – it felt like capitulation to allow Shawn to go with her – but ultimately she gave in. "Fine. This week is all about compromise, right?"

"Right."

Zander smirked as he carried a platter of pancakes toward the table. "I like this idea. It's kind of like you guys will be having a Zander Pritchett Fan Club Meeting. Which one of you is going to be president?"

Jared didn't want to laugh, but he couldn't help himself. He ran his hand down the back of Harper's hair as he sat next to her and pressed a kiss to her forehead. "Isn't this nice?" he asked, beaming. "We're one big, happy family and everything worked out."

"For now," Zander said. "That's only going to last until PMS strikes and you know it."

"We'll take it one step at a time."

"I'M SORRY you got stuck with this."

Harper was excited to spend time with Shawn without Zander and Jared looking over her shoulders, but she felt guilty he was forced into action because Zander and Jared were worrywarts.

"It's fine," Shawn said, his smile genuine. "It gives you and me a chance to get to know one another better. I've been dying to meet you for weeks. You're the lead heroine in every one of Zander's stories."

Harper, her hair pulled back in a ponytail to beat the heat, tilted her head to the side. "I feel a little stupid for not realizing what was going on. Zander was spending even more time at the gym than usual and he was disappearing on errands a lot more frequently than before. It just didn't occur to me."

"Because he always tells you everything?"

"Yeah. He tells me things I don't want to know all of the time. I never thought he would keep something I did want to know from me."

"Please don't hold that against him." Shawn's expression was earnest as he followed Harper down the trail. "He loves you. He was just … confused."

"And what about you?" Harper asked. "Were you confused?"

"I knew I really liked him but wasn't sure how things would shake out," Shawn said. "He's very attached to you and something of a free spirit. I don't know if you know this, but … um … he has a certain reputation around this area."

"Oh, I know," Harper intoned, shaking her head so her ponytail swished. "He's the love 'em and leave 'em type … and he often leaves in dramatic fashion while climbing through a window or making up an outrageous lie. That was the way he operated for years … until you."

"We've only been dating a few weeks," Shawn reminded her. "I think you're giving me more power than I can legitimately claim."

"And I think you're selling yourself short," Harper countered, grinning as she twisted off the water bottle cap. "You seem to be a calm soul. Zander needs that. Jared is a calm soul and he balances me out.

"Zander and I, on the other hand, are theatrical souls," she continued. "We react with our emotions instead of our heads. Jared almost always reacts with his head. It's nice because he doesn't allow us to run off before thinking through our actions."

"Are you saying you haven't found trouble since Jared came into your life?" Shawn asked, his tone light and teasing. "If you are, I'm going to be blunt and say I don't believe you. I heard about the dentist thing."

"No, we'll always find trouble," Harper said, chuckling. "He simply makes us examine a path before we take it. We might still take it despite the danger, but Jared is a calming influence. I think you are, too."

"From you, I'll take that as a compliment. I've seen the way you look at Jared and you think he can do no wrong. It's extremely … sweet."

"He's not perfect," Harper countered. "Did Zander tell you about the time he went home right after we started dating and he didn't call for more than a week?"

"He did," Shawn confirmed, grinning. "He said he considered driving over to the west side of the state to beat up Jared but ultimately decided to eat cookie dough with you instead."

Harper giggled. "He tells you a lot of stories, huh?"

"He loves talking about you. Er, well, he loves talking in general. He has a special glow when he's talking about you, though. I think you guys are adorable."

"I think we know how to push each other's buttons but always show up when the other needs us," Harper clarified. "The thing is … ." Harper broke off and bit her lip.

"Go ahead and say it," Shawn prodded. "We're going to be spending a lot of time together – at least I hope we're going to be doing that – and I want you to feel comfortable with me. I know that's something that happens over time, but the last thing I want is for you to censor yourself."

"Okay." Harper sucked in a calming breath. "I like you. I think you're going to be good for him. You seem so calm and even and yet still exciting. That's exactly what Zander needs.

"I'm a little worried, though," she continued. "Zander has never really been in a long-term relationship. I probably shouldn't be telling you that – it's breaking like ten rules in the best friend ethics book – but I want you to be aware that dating Zander isn't going to be a walk in the park."

"Or to the river," Shawn teased. "Harper, I know he's got some issues. He's unbelievably dramatic. If you could've heard him after he found out you'd been spying on him … well, he had Susan Lucci beat for every daytime Emmy out there."

Harper bit the inside of her cheek to keep from laughing. Every time Shawn opened his mouth she liked him more and more.

"I know he hasn't had a real relationship and I know that you and Zander formed your own club for a lot of years," Shawn said. "I still want to know him, be with him. I still want to give this a chance.

"I can't make any guarantees," he continued. "No one can. I have faith this is going to work out, though. I like to think of myself as a patient man. I also think I'm a little boring because I don't take enough risks.

"You said that Jared and I balance out you and Zander because you're wacky," he said. "The reverse is also true. You balance us out. We need your light to make us happy."

"Oh, I think I'm already in love with you," Harper said, taking Shawn by surprise and throwing her arms around his neck. "You are perfect."

Shawn chuckled as he rubbed her back. "Just don't tell Zander you're in love with me, okay? He might get jealous. For that matter, don't tell Jared either. I own a gym and yet I'm pretty sure he could take me."

Harper chuckled, delighted. "It's going to be okay. You can trust me."

"I already do."

TWENTY-ONE

"You look like you're in a good mood." Mel dropped a doughnut on the corner of Jared's desk and kept walking toward his, an added spring in his step as he clutched his favorite bear claw treat in his hand. "Did you have a nice double date with Zander and his new friend?"

"Friend?" Jared cocked an amused eyebrow. "His name is Shawn. He's very nice. I like him a great deal."

"That's good." Mel looked uncomfortable with the conversational course. "Are they like … spending the night together?"

"Would that bother you?"

"No. I hardly think Zander is a monk. I've heard the stories. I accept him for who he is. I love him no matter what."

"But?"

"It's just got to be weird," Mel said, his cheeks coloring. "You and Harper in one room and Zander and his friend in another. How do you guys swing that?"

"His name is Shawn and you're going to like him," Jared said. "He's extremely calm, which is exactly the type of boyfriend Zander needs. As for the rest, it's not a big deal. Harper has her room and Zander is across the hallway. It's not an issue."

"Calm?" Mel rolled his neck until it cracked. "So it's kind of like Zander is dating you. Er, well, for the most part. You've had a freakout or two, but you're usually the level-headed one in that mess."

"I think that's a compliment and that's exactly how I'm going to take it," Jared said. "And, yes, Shawn is kind of like me. He doesn't melt down at the drop of a hat and he seems to enjoy the mayhem Zander and Harper bring to a relationship."

"So … do you think they'll get married?"

Jared's eyebrows flew up his forehead. "They've been dating for three weeks. I think it's a bit early for that."

"Yeah, but you always know," Mel said. "I knew by the second date that I was going to marry my wife. I'm sure you knew with Harper, too."

Jared shifted on his chair, averting his gaze. "Harper and I have only been dating for a few months. We're not talking about marriage."

"And that's wise. That doesn't mean you're not thinking about it."

Jared balked. "I haven't been thinking about marriage. Why would you even say something like that?"

"Because I see the way you look at her," Mel replied. "You love her. You might not have told her yet – and if you haven't, what are you waiting for? – but you love her. You can't imagine planning a future with anyone but her."

Jared rubbed his chin, his stomach flipping at the notion. Despite his initial reaction to Mel's suggestion, he found that the idea of marriage wasn't altogether frightening. That didn't mean he was going to push things when it was completely unnecessary. "Marriage is down the line."

"Fine."

"Far down the line."

Mel held up his hands in a placating manner. "Fine."

"I am considering trying to figure out a new living arrangement in the next few months, though," Jared admitted. "I love Zander, don't get me wrong, but I would like some privacy. If Zander and Shawn keep going, I would think he'd eventually like some privacy, too."

"So, what's the problem? Are you worried Harper won't leave Zander, or are you afraid Zander will pitch a righteous fit if you even suggest it?"

"Both."

Mel barked out a laugh, genuinely amused. "Well, that's a pickle you've got yourself in. It will all work out, though. I have faith in that."

"I hope so." Jared shook his head and forced himself to return to business. "I'm putting everything together on the Hilliard case. Farber isn't comfortable naming a cause of death. He says he just can't be sure. He is comfortable calling it murder, but he doesn't have a manner for us."

"It's not the end of the world," Mel said. "Just forward what we have to the prosecutor."

"That's what I'm doing now. I'm just going through everything one more time."

"SO ... WHAT do we do?"

Shawn considered himself a brave man under most circumstances – meaning he wasn't afraid of spiders or public speaking, for the most part – but he felt as if he was at a complete loss as he watched Harper pace around the small area where Tess's body was discovered. The police tape remained despite the location being cleared, but Harper barely noticed it as she wandered around the clearing.

"We wait for Tess," Harper replied. "I don't know what else to do."

"How long do you think it will take?"

"You don't have to wait here with me," Harper offered. "I'll be fine. Jared and Zander have mother hen tendencies at times. I'm really in no danger."

"It's okay," Shawn said hurriedly. "I want to stay with you. It's just … I've never seen a ghost before."

"You probably won't see one now," Harper pointed out. "Zander never does. He's witnessed quite a few flying objects and screeches, but he's never seen a ghost."

"I can't decide if that makes me feel better or is somehow disappointing."

Harper snickered. "For the most part, the bulk of ghost interactions I've been a part of are boring. I don't expect this one to be exciting, if that makes you feel better."

"So you'll just tell Tess what you've found out and hope she passes over?"

"Basically."

"That doesn't sound so bad," Shawn said, stretching his legs out as he sat on a rock and stared at the river. "This is a really pretty place. What's the house like?"

"It's a Victorian and you can tell it was once quite beautiful. It's falling apart now, though. I'm betting that Matthew will get a good offer on it despite that. It's a unique parcel with the river and everything."

"What about you? Would you like a house like that?"

"I'm not afraid of the work, but I think the house is too big. I prefer something smaller, homier even. I used to think I wanted a big house, but now I'm pretty sure I want something more manageable."

"That makes sense."

Harper shifted her eyes to Shawn and found him staring off into space, his mind clearly busy. "Are you worried about our living arrangements?"

"No." Shawn immediately shook his head but Harper read the guilt in his eyes. That's exactly what he'd been thinking about. She was sure of it. "I think your house is neat."

"It's okay," Harper said, bending over so she could scoop up a rock and skip it toward the river. The water ran slowly in this area so she actually managed to get the stone to skip twice before sinking. "I've been thinking about the arrangement lately, too."

"You have?" Shawn looked almost relieved. "I don't want to push anything and I'm perfectly happy with the way things are right now. Down the road, though ... ."

"Down the road we're going to have issues," Harper finished. "I've figured that out myself, too. I don't know what to do about it. When Zander and I bought the house it felt like an easy fit. It never occurred to me that things would shift the way they have.

"I know we can't live together forever, but I'm honestly going to miss him," she continued. "Jared deserves some peace of mind, though. Of course, I don't know how I'm supposed to broach the subject of us living together."

"You don't have to do anything right away," Shawn reminded her. "You have plenty of time. Just think about things, decide what you really want, and then ask him what he wants. I'm going to bet he's given some thought to the living arrangements, too."

"You're probably right." Harper heaved out a sigh. "It's weird to think that a year from now things might be really different. It's exciting and scary at the same time."

Shawn smirked. "I think life is exciting and scary at the same time no matter how you look at it."

"You have a point." Harper bent over to gather another stone and then straightened as she focused on the tree next to the spot where Tess's body was discovered. She wasn't surprised to find the taciturn ghost staring back at her. "There you are, Tess. We've been looking for you."

WHAT IS this?" Jared held up an aged datebook and waved it to get Mel's attention.

"Oh, that's a pile of stuff Matthew Fleming dropped off," Mel replied. "He stopped by right before I locked the office yesterday. It's journals belonging to his mother. He thought they might be of some help. Apparently they're dated and everything. He found them in the attic."

Jared's eyebrows winged up. "Is there anything in here about Tess?"

Mel shrugged. "I didn't look. Honestly, I forgot all about them. I'm not sure if they're going to be able to help."

"Well, it can't hurt to look." Jared heaved out a sigh. "You could help if you wanted to make this go faster, by the way."

"Oh, what a sweet offer," Mel intoned. "I think I'm happy with my doughnut, though."

"You suck."

"Yes, but I've got seniority," Mel reminded him. "That means I'm the boss of suck to you."

"Good to know."

WHO ARE you?"

Tess's voice was weak, watery almost, and she seemed just as surprised as Harper when she opened her mouth and sound came out.

"My name is Harper Harlow. I'm … something of a spirit sensitive. I guess that's the best way to explain it."

Tess's face remained blank.

"That means I can see and talk to ghosts," Harper supplied, adopting a gentle tone. "I've seen you a few times now. I wanted to talk to you yesterday but … well … I didn't think it was a good idea considering everything that was going on."

"You can talk to ghosts?"

"I … yes." Something terrible occurred to Harper. "You do know you're dead, right?"

Tess chuckled, the sound low and unnatural. "Yes. I'm well aware that I'm dead. I watched my body decompose in this spot for a very long time."

"Have you been here this entire time? Alone?"

"Yes. There was nowhere else to go and no one ever came to visit."

Harper's heart rolled. She expected that answer, but it still hurt to hear it. "I'm sorry. That must've been a lonely existence. If I'd known you were out here I would've come sooner."

"What is she saying?" Shawn whispered, gripping his knees tightly as he sat. "Is she threatening to eat us?"

"She's not a zombie," Harper said dryly.

"I know. Ghosts eat people, too."

"They do not."

"I saw it on television."

Harper rolled her eyes. "You have a dramatic side, too. Don't let anyone tell you differently." She turned back to Tess. "Do you know what happened to you?"

"I died."

"I mean … do you know how?"

"Things kind of melt together," Tess mused as she tilted her head to the side. "My memories are jumbled. I know that Arthur told me it was over and that I had to move on. I remember that very clearly. I was angry like you wouldn't believe and told him he would never see the baby again. He said he didn't care and I was … furious."

"I can understand that." Harper opted to take a sympathetic stance. "Arthur got you pregnant. He owed your son a proper upbringing. He owed Joshua a good life. That was his responsibility and it wasn't right of him to turn his back on that."

"Joshua?" Tess took on a wistful look.

"I haven't seen him personally, but I have seen photographs," Harper offered. "Madison adopted him. She raised him as her own. He had a good education and she loves him dearly. I'm sure it wasn't the same as growing up with you, but he's okay. You don't have to worry about him."

"No offense, but I never worried about Joshua," Tess said. "I suppose I loved him … in my own way, of course. He was my son. How could I not love him?"

"I don't know," Harper answered honestly.

"I wanted Arthur more," Tess said. "He's the entire reason I got pregnant with Joshua in the first place. I wanted us to be a family. I wanted that house … and that life … and that man."

"That was never going to happen." Harper was sympathetic to Tess's plight, but it was clear the spirit needed a hard dose of reality. "The house was Annette's no matter what. It was left to her through her family. Arthur had no claim on it and he knew it. He signed a prenuptial agreement."

"What?" Tess's already ethereal face got even whiter, if that was even possible. "That can't be right."

"I'm sorry, but it is," Harper explained. "Arthur had very little money and if he'd chosen to divorce Annette, he would've had even less. The house belonged to Annette and Arthur would've had to pay spousal support. That was clearly something he didn't want to do."

"But … that's not how I imagined things." Tess was like a petulant child who just now realized Santa Claus wasn't real.

"I'm sorry you're disappointed, but that's the reason Arthur stayed even though he and Annette clearly hated each other," Harper said. "Did Arthur kill you because you were pressuring him?"

"Arthur loved me."

That wasn't an answer, but Harper didn't want to press the spirit too hard. She seemed shaky. If she disappeared, there was no telling when she would return. "Tell me the last thing you remember," she prodded. "Where were you?"

"I was at home," Tess said, shifting as she floated, her eyes falling on the river. "I was upset. Arthur had just broken up with me for like the thirtieth time. I knew it wouldn't last – it never did – but I was sick of playing his games.

"I called Madison and asked her to watch Joshua," she continued. "She agreed. She even said she wanted Joshua to live with her full time and she would take care of everything. I considered it, but that weakened my position with Arthur so I told her I needed more time to make my decision.

"I got in the car and drove to the house." She pressed her eyes shut as she searched her memory. "It was raining, but I didn't care. I decided I was going to confront Annette myself. I was going to tell her about the affair … about Joshua … and then I was going to demand she let Arthur go."

"Don't you think that was a bit presumptuous?" Harper challenged. "For better or for worse, Arthur and Annette were married. He belonged to her. How could you make demands?"

"Because he loved me."

"But did you love him?"

Tess seemed surprised by the question. "What do you mean?"

"I'm asking if you loved him," Harper said, her voice firm. "I'm going to be honest. I don't think you did. I think you wanted him to give you a specific life, but I don't think you loved him."

"Does that really matter now?"

"I guess not," Harper conceded. "I just can't figure out why you thought it was a good idea to force Arthur's hand. It's long since in the past, though. What happened?"

"I can't rightly recall," Tess replied, her tone noticeably chillier. She obviously didn't like Harper judging her. "I got out of the car and the rain was coming down in buckets. The driveway was muddy and I slipped. I could hear yelling inside … it was, well, I can't remember who it was. I do know they were screaming at each other, though. It was an extremely loud and violent fight.

"I remember thinking that it was a good sign and even though it was raining like crazy I stopped on the front porch to listen," she continued. "They were going at each other pretty good and then … it got silent. I think someone stormed out of the room. That's when the door opened and … that's it. That's all I can remember."

"You don't remember who opened the door?" Harper couldn't help but be frustrated.

"It must've been Annette, right? Arthur would never hurt me and whoever opened that door hurt me."

"I guess." Harper rubbed the back of her neck. "It would be so much easier if you could remember. It would help you move on. It would put the past to rest."

"I remember."

Harper stilled at the new voice, swiveling slowly to her left and frowning when she caught sight of a familiar figure. "Annette?"

The elderly woman nodded as she stepped into the clearing. She looked … dazed. Harper couldn't think of another way to describe her.

"Did you kill her?" Harper asked, resigned.

"Of course not," another voice answered from the shadows behind Annette. "She didn't even open the door."

TWENTY-TWO

For one wild moment Harper thought Arthur's ghost was going to make an appearance. She didn't know why she felt that way, but it almost seemed poetic. Perhaps Tess and Arthur would be able to have a long overdue showdown after all. Maybe she would get the closure she so desperately needed.

Instead Matthew Fleming moved into the clearing behind his mother, a gun in his hand, and the look he fixed Harper with was decidedly deadly.

"Hello, Ms. Harlow."

Harper's heart caught in her throat as Shawn scrambled to his feet behind her.

"What's going on?" Shawn sounded breathless, his voice strangled.

Harper had no idea how to answer. "I don't … know."

"Oh, really?" Matthew cocked a challenging eyebrow. "You don't know what's going on? I thought you were supposed to be smart. Haven't you been working on this case with the police? Aren't you some sort of expert?"

Harper swallowed hard. Matthew looked angry. Actually, he was bordering on deranged. She couldn't wrap her head around the scenario. "I only accompanied Jared because he thought Annette would respond better to me than him," she lied. "He thought she would prefer a friendly female face."

"You delivered that quite well," Matthew said. "For some reason I don't believe you, though."

"I don't understand what's going on," Shawn hedged, protectively moving to Harper's side. He rested a hand on her arm, offering comfort, but never moved his eyes from Matthew's face. "Why do you have a gun?"

"And why are you out walking through the woods with your elderly mother?" Harper added. "She shouldn't be exerting so much energy. It's hot out here. She could get easily dehydrated and … ."

Matthew waited a moment, as if daring Harper to continue. "Almost as if she could get dehydrated and lose her way? Perhaps fall in the river? Oh, why didn't I think of that? Doh!"

Matthew's tone was chilly and Harper couldn't help but inadvertently shudder.

"I remember what happened now," Tess intoned, her gaze glazed. "I remember how I died."

"HERE'S SOMETHING." Jared leaned forward at his desk, his index finger busy as it moved back and forth down an old day planner.

"What do you have?" Mel asked, legitimately curious. Despite his earlier reticence he grabbed a handful of journals and proceeded to read them with his feet propped up on his desk. "According to the missing person report Madison filed, Tess disappeared on the weekend of June 20th."

"So?"

"On the weekend of June 20th Annette was over in Ann Arbor for a church festival," Jared replied. "She was gone overnight."

"Let me check the journals," Mel said, flipping through notebooks until he found the one he wanted. "Here we go." He was silent as he read for several minutes, his eyes going wide at some point. "Um, okay. I definitely found something here."

"What?"

"Annette left town all right. She was glad to be away from Whisper Cove because she knew Arthur was going to break up with Tess. They had a long talk and he agreed to do it. She didn't want to be around for the fallout."

"Okay, that must mean Arthur killed Tess," Jared mused. "He was the only one home that weekend. That makes me feel a little better. At least Annette won't be getting away with murder."

"No, but Arthur wasn't alone," Mel said, his expression grave. "Annette wrote that Matthew was there at the time, even staying at the house even though he had his own apartment. He promised to help his father deal with the Tess situation and clean out the house to make sure none of her things were around for Annette to stumble across.

"Apparently Annette issued an ultimatum," he continued. "She told Arthur to make sure that Tess didn't have any reason to visit. She made Matthew stay with his father to make sure it was done correctly."

Jared tilted his head to the side, considering. "That can't be right. Matthew said he had no idea who Tess was."

"Not according to this."

"But … if that's right, that means … ." Jared's heart painfully rolled as he pushed himself to his feet. "That means Matthew has been lying to us from the beginning."

"But why? Why not admit that his father killed Tess? He was an adult at the time, but he could hardly be blamed for what happened."

"Unless he could," Jared said, his heart rate increasing. "What if Arthur didn't kill Tess at all? What if it was Matthew?"

"But ... why?"

"Maybe to protect his mother. Maybe to protect his father. Or maybe to protect himself. Madison said that Tess made an offhand joke about seducing Matthew as a form of punishment for Arthur. What if that really happened?"

"Then Matthew was probably a pretty messed up dude."

"And that messed up dude is at the house ... while Harper is right behind the house talking to a ghost."

"You don't think she's in danger, do you?" Mel wasn't nearly as worried as Jared. "He wouldn't dare go after Harper."

"He would if he thought she knew his big secret." Jared reached for his keys. "She's probably fine but ... ."

Mel blew out a sigh. "I'm coming with you."

"Good."

"You guys are so dramatic, though. Has anyone ever told you that?"

"I can live with the drama. I can't live without her. Come on. My stomach is in knots. I don't like this."

"IT WAS Matthew."

Tess's voice was ominous and Harper almost believed the spirit would shed a tear ... if that were physically possible.

"He opened the door," Tess said. "He saw me standing there. He knew I'd been listening. He knew ... oh, he knew that I'd chosen his father over him. I told him that was a possibility, but he always refused to listen. He had stars in his eyes, that boy. He never understood the importance of being pragmatic."

Harper pressed the heel of her hand to her forehead as the final pieces of the puzzle slipped into place. Neither Arthur nor Annette had killed Tess. They were wrong from the beginning. That didn't mean it wasn't a family affair.

"You killed Tess." The words were out of Harper's mouth before she had a chance to consider the intelligence associated with uttering them. "You were having an affair with her, too."

Annette's eyes widened at the pronouncement. "No." She was aghast as she glanced over her shoulder and glared at her son. The confused fog that rested on her shoulders only minutes before was gone. "You, too? How could you?"

"Don't look at me that way," Matthew spat, the hand holding the gun shaking. "She was mine. We were destined to be together. I loved her."

"I thought you said you left town before your father and Tess took up with one another," Harper prodded. "That was obviously a lie."

"He was still in the house," Tess offered. "He followed his father one night and discovered the affair. He pounded on my door afterward, accusing me of trying to ruin his family. He was really angry and I was a little bit worried about him opening his big mouth so I did the only thing I could do."

Harper's stomach twisted at the visual. "Oh, geez."

"Oh, geez, what?" Matthew wrinkled his nose. "Oh, don't look so high and mighty. My father was a user and abuser. I wanted to make a real life with Tess. I wanted us to have the sort of future we could only dream about as long as she was hung up on an old man who could offer her nothing. I was ready to give up everything for her."

"But what about your father?"

"What about him? He was always a mean prick. He didn't love me. He didn't respect me. If it came to a choice between Tess and him, well, there was no choice. Tess won hands down."

"Only she didn't win," Harper reminded him. "No one won. She was too fixated on your father. She thought if she stuck with him she'd end up with the house and the status. She even had a baby in the hope of trapping him. That must've rubbed you the wrong way."

"It did," Matthew confirmed. "Especially since that was my baby."

Harper stilled, her eyes briefly flicking to Tess for confirmation. For her part, the ghost merely looked interested in the conversation. There was no guilt or remorse emanating from her.

"If Tess was sleeping with both you and your father, how did you know the baby was yours?" Harper asked.

"Because my father had a vasectomy after my sister's birth," Matthew replied. "He didn't want more children. He and my mother had separate bedrooms but occasionally they would jump each other after a particularly vicious fight. Don't ask me why."

Harper made a face, the visual repulsing her. "Okay."

"My mother also knew that my father was running around on her," Matthew added. "She didn't want a woman showing up pregnant so my father agreed to have a vasectomy. That was their … compromise."

"Is that true?" Harper asked, focusing on Annette.

"I didn't care who he had sex with. I simply didn't want to be responsible for any mistakes," Annette replied stiffly. "I'm not proud of how things went down, but I was raised to believe that you marry for better or worse. Divorce wasn't an option."

"Oh, Annette." Harper made a clucking sound as she shook her head. "Everyone deserves a shot at a happy life."

"It's too late now," Annette replied. "It was too late then. I didn't know about the other, though. I didn't know about Matthew. I would've killed her myself if I did. I promise you that."

"So what happened?" Harper asked, locking gazes with Matthew. "You knocked up Tess and yet she told everyone Arthur was the father. That must've ticked you off."

"I had a lot of patience with her," Matthew said. "I knew she was trying to wrap her head around a few things and I went out of my way to explain them. She wouldn't listen, though."

"Arthur was the father of my baby," Tess snapped. "Do you think I don't know the father of my own baby?"

There was something about the way she said it that made Harper's stomach twist.

"Why do you keep looking over there?" Matthew asked, annoyed. "Do you see something over there?"

Harper decided to play the only card she had in her deck. "It's Tess."

"Tess?" Matthew laughed hollowly. "Tess is dead. She was buried long ago and the only reason any of this is happening is because my mother took it upon herself to search the attic. I told you to wait for me, you old bat!"

Annette cringed at the tone of his voice, but she didn't shrink away from him. Despite her age and frailty, she refused to give anyone the satisfaction of beating her. "It's my house. I'm allowed to clean my house."

"That doesn't mean you're allowed to take my personal property, my photos, to the police," Matthew seethed. "You caused all of this. She would've stayed dead and buried forever if you hadn't gone to the cops. What is wrong with you?"

Harper wasn't thrilled with Annette's attitude but there was no way she could allow Matthew to keep talking to his mother in that manner. "Leave her alone," Harper said, jerking forward and reaching for Annette's hand. "There's no reason to abuse her."

Matthew slapped away Harper's hand and glowered at her. "Don't push me. This is as much your fault as it is anyone else's."

"That's rich," Harper shot back. "How do you figure that?"

"Because everyone knows you pretend to see ghosts for money," Matthew shot back. "Your father must be mortified. The great Phil Harlow, one of the most popular guys in school, has a complete and total whackjob as a daughter. The shame he lives with must be terrible."

"Hey!" Shawn was incensed on Harper's behalf.

"It's okay," Harper said, patting his arm. "That's hardly important given the circumstances."

"You've got that right," Matthew intoned, annoyed. "It's definitely your fault, though. My mother made the first mistake by taking those photographs to the police. I wasn't particularly worried, though. All of this could easily be blamed on my father.

"Then you and your little boyfriend kept snooping around," he continued. "It wasn't bad enough that you stole Tess's body. I wanted her on my property. I wanted her where only I could get to her. Only my father and I knew where we buried her and I had plans to move to this house and be with her forever once I divorced my wife and got my mother out of here. You ruined that.

"You also just had to visit Madison, too, didn't you?" he said. "I followed you that day. I saw you talking to her. I knew then I was in trouble if you guys ran a DNA test. The results would come back close but not as an exact match. That threw everything into turmoil."

"We had no intention of running a DNA test," Harper said smoothly. "It wasn't part of our plan."

"Well, I couldn't know that," Matthew said. "I thought you would focus on my father and let it go. You didn't, though. Then you decided to fixate on my mother. I wasn't thrilled with that, but it was something I could deal with. I led you right to the answers and you ignored them."

"Because we wanted justice for Tess," Harper replied. "We wanted Tess to be able to move on."

Matthew guffawed loudly. "Move on? Where is she supposed to move on to? Good grief. She's dead. She's been dead for twenty-five years. I slammed her head into the door frame when she wouldn't listen to me and then forced my father to help me bury her."

Harper glanced at Tess and found the woman's already shaky figure fading. Would she run away again? "So your father knew you killed Tess and instead of turning you in he helped you? That was nice of him."

"He didn't want anyone finding out that we both slept with the same woman. He thought it was embarrassing. Like it wasn't embarrassing for him to run around on my mother!"

"Do you mean the mother you forced to march through the woods in ninety-degree heat with the intention of drowning her in the river?" Harper had no idea why she pushed so hard, but Matthew's oblivious nature and refusal to take any responsibility had her at her wit's end. "Is that what you mean?"

Annette pressed her eyes shut and shook her head as Shawn gasped.

"Harper." Shawn's voice was low and full of warning. "What are you going to do?"

"Yes, Harper, what are you going to do?" Matthew gritted out, his lips twisted into an ugly sneer.

"I think the better question is: What are *you* going to do?" Harper challenged. "I have several people who know where I am. They know where I parked and exactly why I was coming out here.

"You have a problem," she continued. "You have your mother, Shawn, and me to account for. Do you really think you're going to be able to pull that off? I'm guessing your plan was to force your mother to march around out here until she passed out. Then you were going to drag her into the river and make sure she drowned. That would be a convenient accidental death for you. A veritable tragedy given her fragile mental state.

"There's no way that's going to work for all of us and we know what you've done," she said. "Think really long and hard about what you're doing here, Matthew. This is already over. It's already done. You can either make things worse or you can give up and accept your punishment."

TWENTY-THREE

Jared let himself in Harper's house shortly before midnight. He was exhausted. The fallout from Matthew's shooting took longer than he expected. Even though it was an open-and-shut case, the sheriff's department conducted a review. The interview took four hours, but by the time he left the office it had been declared a clean shoot.

Harper and Shawn were questioned, too, although their interviews were brief and the sheriff's department cut them loose relatively quickly. Harper didn't want to leave, but Jared knew he wouldn't be able to focus on the review if she stayed. Finally they compromised and he promised to arrive at her house as soon as possible … and spend a day hammocking by the river over the weekend. Neither was much of a sacrifice.

He found Harper, Zander, and Shawn zonked out on the couch. Harper, her flaxen hair falling out of her ponytail holder, was buffered between the two of them. Jared took the time to snap a photograph with his phone before pocketing it. The two men looked as if they were trying to protect her from both sides while she slept. No nightmares would make it past their barriers if they had anything to say about it.

He slipped his arms beneath her legs and quietly tried to remove her from the huddle, but Zander stirred, his eyes flashing when he registered movement in the room. Jared pressed a finger to his lips.

"Don't wake her," he whispered.

"I have no intention of waking her," Zander replied, his voice low. "It took forever to get her to settle down.

What happened? Are you in trouble for shooting Matthew? If so, I'll go to court to testify if you need it. I always fancied myself a star on *Perry Mason* reruns."

Jared didn't bother to hide his smirk. "You weren't there."

"I was in spirit."

Jared was absurdly touched by the sentiment. "It's okay. The sheriff's department cleared me. Matthew's body is at the medical examiner's office and his wife is on her way to town to claim it."

"What about Annette?"

"She was lucid for about an hour after the shooting and then she became forgetful. I'm not sure if that was real or something she made up because she was tired of answering questions. I guess it doesn't really matter."

"Did she know they killed Tess?"

"She suspected that Arthur killed her," Jared replied. "She didn't know that for a fact, though. She said that she was suspicious when she heard Tess disappeared. It wasn't a big story, but it was the talk of the town for a few days. She thought he did it for her. Ironically, she said that made her hate him more. She couldn't rightly explain why."

"I think that marriage was more complicated than anyone thought," Zander said. "Perhaps there was real love there, or at least attraction. I guess we'll never know."

"Probably not. As for the photographs, she didn't remember bringing them to us. I think her memory is well and truly shot."

"What will happen to Annette now?" Zander asked. "Will she be able to stay in her house?"

"I doubt it. The two daughters have been called. They're coming to town to deal with it. Mel is staying on the couch tonight so Annette isn't alone. She seemed … confused … when it was all said and done. She kept asking to talk to Matthew."

"She never knew he was sleeping with Tess, too?"

"She said she had no idea. She said she would've killed Tess herself had she known. We really only got an hour to question her before things fell apart."

"Will you try again?"

Jared shrugged. "I don't see the point. We know what happened. Matthew's been punished. Annette, whatever her faults, didn't murder anyone. Heck, Arthur didn't murder anyone. He simply helped his son bury a body."

"That must've been a hard secret to keep," Zander mused, rubbing his chin. "They didn't like each other as it was and then they had to cover up a murder together. I can't imagine that helped the relationship."

"I'm guessing nothing was going to help any of the relationships," Jared said, his fingers gentle as they pushed a strand of Harper's hair out of her face. "She's really out of it. Is she okay?"

"She was a little shaken up. She had a lot of nervous energy. She was sad that you were forced to kill on her behalf … again."

"I didn't kill on her behalf. I made sure she wasn't killed by someone else. I protected and served … just like I was supposed to do."

"You're still a hero. You're my hero as well as her hero."

Jared pursed his lips and shook his head. "You have a really good heart and always know the right thing to say at the oddest times."

"I'm a magical man." Zander's grin was impish as he stretched. "So are, too. You're magical to her and that's the most important thing. You know that, right?"

"I know that I adore her."

"I know that, too." Zander shifted his eyes to Shawn. "I should get him to bed."

"How is he?" Jared asked, his eyes drifting to his left. "This had to be a big deal for him. It's not every day you walk to the river with a ghost hunter and watch a man die."

"He seems … conflicted," Zander replied. "I think he'll be okay, though. He needs sleep."

"You should know that when the gun went off he threw himself on top of Harper to protect her. He's a hero, too."

"That doesn't surprise me," Zander said. "You can tell a man's heart by looking into his eyes. That's where the soul lives."

"Oh, you're feeling poetic tonight," Jared teased, sliding his arms under Harper's legs. "No offense, but I'm tired. I'm taking my Heart to bed. Don't even think of climbing in there with us tomorrow morning."

"You're getting her naked?" Zander was affronted.

Jared scorched him with a murderous look. "Not tonight."

"You'd better not."

"Tomorrow is another story." Jared smirked at Zander's outraged expression as he cradled Harper in his arms and strode toward her bedroom. "Omelets sound good for breakfast tomorrow," he called out in a stage whisper. "I want mushrooms in mine."

"You're a demanding guy."

"That's one of the perks of being a hero. You should know."

Zander watched him go, a small smile playing at the corner of his lips. At one time he thought he would be crushed when Harper finally found the perfect hero. It turned out they both fell in love with him at the same time – just in different ways.

Made in the USA
Lexington, KY
15 January 2017